ADA MONCRIEFF

Ada Moncrieff is the author of *Murder Most Festive*.
She lives and works in London.

ALSO BY ADA MONCRIEFF

Murder Most Festive

ADA MONCRIEFF

Murder at the Theatre Royale

VINTAGE

1 3 5 7 9 10 8 6 4 2

Vintage is part of the Penguin Random House group of companies
whose addresses can be found at global.penguinrandomhouse.com

Penguin
Random House
UK

First published by Vintage in 2022

penguin.co.uk/vintage

A CIP catalogue record for this book is available from the British Library

ISBN 9781529115314

Typeset in 11/15.75pt Stempel Garamond LT Std
by Jouve (UK), Milton Keynes.
Printed and bound in Great Britain by Clays Ltd, Elcograf S.p.A.

The authorised representative in the EEA is Penguin Random House Ireland,
Morrison Chambers, 32 Nassau Street, Dublin D02 YH68

Penguin Random House is committed to a sustainable future
for our business, our readers and our planet. This book is made
from Forest Stewardship Council® certified paper.

MIX
Paper from
responsible sources
FSC® C018179

Men's courses will foreshadow certain ends, to
which, if persevered in, they must lead.

Charles Dickens, *A Christmas Carol*

1

The December sky had, for some six days, been spitting sleet at the London streets and spitefully hurling hailstones at those brave – or foolish – enough to be jostling along the pavements in search of the perfect Christmas gift. On this particular day, however, December 22nd, the firmament appeared to have exhausted its ill will towards the denizens of the city. Instead, it was bestowing upon London that most seasonal of offerings: a blindingly pristine blanket of snow. The flakes settled upon the windowpanes of the *Daily Chronicle*'s offices, within which typewriters trilled and conversations – some hushed, others weary, a great many others deliciously trifling – burbled.

One such conversation was occurring in the office occupied by Editor-in-Chief Martin Halliday, although, regrettably for its participants, the discussion was bereft of trifles and laden with labour. The combatants sat – one slouching in a posture which conveyed the inconvenience of the protracted dialogue, the other perched uncomfortably in a stance designed to project professionalism and composure – on opposing sides of a great mahogany desk. Strewn with a wild disorder of editions old and new and a miscellany of unexplained trinkets (the magnifying glass and the feather had always provoked the most puzzlement), the desk had borne the weight of its fair share of tête-à-têtes between Halliday and disgruntled employees. At this moment, however, it was bearing witness to a conversation whose repercussions would be felt for many years to come.

'King, it's nothing personal – Jenkins is just a newspaperman through and through, like a stick of Brighton rock,' Martin Halliday explained, idly flicking an elastic band in his left hand, swiping some mince pie crumbs from his desk with his right. 'That hoo-ha with the laundry workers last month – Jenkins had the scoop thanks to his bobby pals. The stiffs who'd popped their clogs in Soho – Jenkins was there, had the nod from the squire at the Three Greyhounds. Not to mention he sniffed out that bad apple in Westminster before you could say, "How's yer father?" He's a bloodhound, King, like I said: a newspaperman to his core.'

Daphne King remained silent, eyes fixed on the middle-aged man before her. Arms folded tightly across her blouse, Daphne allowed a flicker of wry amusement to flash across her face. There were a thousand and one things she could have said at that moment, and later she would upbraid herself mercilessly for saying not one of them. Perhaps Martin Halliday would be interested to know that it was *her* contact within the laundry who had apprised her and Jenkins of the scandal that made headlines some weeks ago. Halliday ought really to be aware that *Daphne's* instincts about the Soho murders had sent Jenkins along the path which had led to his front-page splash. Incredulity may be provoked by the knowledge that yes, bravo, *Daphne King's* nose for unsavoury vices was in fact behind the Westminster revelation. It was possible, just possible that Martin Halliday, as editor-in-chief of a national newspaper, might thank Daphne for enlightening him about the true nature of his star reporter. Jamie Jenkins, heavy of brow, light of morals, had spent the last six months swooping like a gangling, ill-fed vulture on any lead that Daphne had foolishly, naively, *idiotically* allowed him access to.

However, instead of regaling her boss with a glorious narrative casting Jenkins as nefarious weasel and she as slighted genius, Daphne sustained her silence. Five years of working for Halliday had provided her with ample evidence that women subsisting on a diet of sour grapes were not popular within the walls – or the pages – of the *Daily Chronicle*. The office Christmas bash the previous evening had been an exercise in self-restraint for Daphne. The backslapping and the bravado among Jamie Jenkins and his cronies was always hard to stomach, but never more so than when accompanied by tepid mulled wine and cold tongue sandwiches. Daphne had stayed just long enough to hear the nauseatingly self-aggrandising speech delivered by Jenkins (unless she was very much mistaken, he had laboriously compared his endless search for truth and justice to the journey of the humble shepherds seeking out the baby Jesus) before hastily glugging down her wine and catching the bus home. From the appearance of both the office and its occupants this morning, the revels had continued for quite some time after Daphne's departure.

Eyes unmistakably bloodshot, and a distinct whiff of brandy wafting across the desk with every laboured breath that he took, Halliday had evidently enjoyed the festivities and was now enduring the consequences. Unkempt moustache somewhat droopy, paunch in evidence as he continued to slouch in his chair, he rummaged restlessly through the newspapers on his desk, before alighting on one particular copy, opening it to a double page and flinging it towards Daphne.

'A newspaper is like a living, breathing animal, King. A tiger, if you will. Like a tiger, all its . . . bits and bobs serve a purpose,' Halliday began. Daphne frowned, wondering what route this analogy would take. 'Now, your news reporters – Jamie and the like – they're your claws, your teeth. Antagonistic, ruthless. Whereas you, Dear Susan, well, you're . . . you're the lovely, warm . . . furry tummy. Comforting, reassuring, cosy.'

Halliday's deftness with metaphors had never been a strength, and this puzzling speech was further evidence of this, if it had been needed. Daphne glanced down at the page he had directed her towards. Page 19, of course: the page dedicated to the *Chronicle*'s ludicrously popular agony aunt, 'Dear Susan'. The role that Daphne had found herself inhabiting for far too long now; what had started as a lark had become something of an albatross. Daphne had surprised herself with the talent she had for dispensing wisdom and guiding her readers towards untangling their conundrums – domestic (how does one dissuade ants from nesting in one's kitchen?), emotional (but what shall I do about Shirley, the new neighbour who keeps inexplicably swapping our milk bottles?), occasionally physical (the bunions still haven't gone!).

It had been the case of the Gambling Contessa that had started the sea change for Daphne. A year ago, perhaps eighteen months, the letters had started to arrive. The tone of voice stilted, peculiar. Nothing Daphne could put her finger on, but nonetheless an inkling: strange turns of phrase here and there, archaic idioms thrown hither and thither. Three a week perhaps, no name at the bottom. The letters weren't coherent enough to warrant publication, but something about them made Daphne hold on to them. Reading and re-reading them, patterns started to emerge: there had been a code there, a message hidden in plain sight. An SOS call. Daphne had put two and two together and realised that the letters were from Lucretia Hallenstrop, aka the Gambling Contessa, aka the Kidnapped Heiress, whose disappearance had been making headlines for weeks. Daphne contacted the police with her findings, and bingo: the mystery of the Gambling Contessa was solved. The heiress later explained that the youngest member of the kidnapping gang – a rather sheepish-looking fellow with a cowlick – had become somewhat smitten with her, and was glamoured into smuggling out her letters in the belief that he was delivering epistles to the contessa's ailing grandmother.

Once word was out that Dear Susan had been in correspondence with Lucretia Hallenstrop, that, in the contessa's own words, 'I've followed her wisdom for years; I knew I could trust her to find me,' the column's popularity became stratospheric. Housewives up and down the country were united in their adoration for Dear Susan, desperate for her counsel. Martin Halliday couldn't believe his luck: he had a gold mine on his hands. Daphne, however, had become increasingly ambivalent about her role. Tracking down Hallenstrop had given her a taste for the thrill of the high-stakes chase. No longer was it enough to advise Barbara of Basingstoke that perhaps the lipstick smudges on her husband's collar were a sign of shenanigans. Daphne's appetite lay in the uncovering of more nefarious deeds. Murderers and thieves and organised thuggery, that's where Daphne King felt she could truly shine.

Daphne glanced at the column in front of her, one which had concerned itself with whether a lunch of cold chicken and claret was an appropriate spread for a visit from one's mother-in-law. Despite the Gambling Contessa cause célèbre, Halliday had refused to budge on his policy about the anonymity of Dear Susan. No byline photo for Daphne, but rather a silhouette of a figure in a jaunty dress hat, martini glass angled in hand. Halliday was of the opinion that Dear Susan ought to remain a figure whose pragmatism was matched by her mystique. In other words, the women of little England should be encouraged to believe that their woes were being pondered by a sympathetic society hostess perhaps skimming their letters in a sun-dappled orangerie, having just been served a light breakfast by her butler, rather than knowing that they were in fact being pored over by an unmarried thirty-seven-year-old renting a room in a Camberwell boarding house. Anonymity it was, then.

'I understand all that, Martin, really I do,' Daphne began, forcing her face to arrange itself into the polite smile that had seen her weather many a storm. 'But, if I may be blunt, Jenkins has been here all of five minutes; I've worked for you for five years—'

'And during those five years you've proved yourself to be a fine little writer, King, really, with a fine little line in no-nonsense advice for all those hopeless housewives and clueless girls who need your help. That mousy little Daphne King from 1930 could barely deliver tea to our desks without spilling it. Wouldn't say boo to a goose. And now look at you. The Daphne King of 1935 has a lovely little way with words; our lady readers would be rampaging around like headless chickens if it weren't for you.' Halliday's voice was wheedling, his wish to be rid of Daphne evident from the numerous glances above her head to where the hour hand on the silver-faced wall clock was nudging eleven.

Daphne's smile had faltered only slightly, accustomed as she was to the repeated association of diminutive adjectives with her career.

'And I've been grateful for all that, Martin, you know I have. But, to be blunt again, I'm a touch . . . well, I feel that I might be in need of a little variety. I'm not quite sure I can muster the enthusiasm to tell one more Maud from Bagshot how to cultivate the perfect begonia, or advise another Gladys of Woolton about what to do if her husband's peculiar about his soufflé. If I'm to advance myself, make a name for myself, like you have –' Daphne knew that the prudent deployment of flattery would reap dividends '– then I need to branch out, spread my wings, add another string to my bow.'

Halliday's elastic band flew across the office and he wagged his finger knowingly at Daphne. 'You see, King, all that lovely flowery language of yours – that's what we need you for. You writing about thugs and lowlifes, badgering barristers for titbits and hounding hoodlums for tip-offs – it just won't wash, I'm afraid. Jenkins gets the promotion, and that's my final word on the matter.'

'Then perhaps . . . perhaps the moment has come for Dear Susan to dust off her valise and part ways with the *Chronicle*.' Daphne fixed her eyes on Halliday's. That this was a dangerous manoeuvre, she could not deny, but Daphne had calculated the risks and concluded that the odds were in her favour. Halliday had built his career through tenacity, pugnacity and not a little duplicity – should the necessity (or rather, opportunity) arise. He proudly lived by a maxim that he was fond of sharing with his employees: a good newspaperman should never be afraid of wading into the muck to get a good story, because a good newspaperman should have a good wife at home to wash that muck out. Ostensibly ill-matched with Halliday's definition of a good newspaperman, Daphne had nevertheless decided that this was the moment to display just how tenacious – and potentially pugnacious – she could be.

Halliday had the disconcerting habit of twiddling his moustache when hungry or nervous, and vestiges of what looked like brown sauce on his collar led Daphne to conclude that he was not yet in the grips of hunger. Nerves it was then. Daphne allowed herself a discreet smile. If Halliday was nervous, that meant that her calculations had been accurate. Dear Susan had accounted for a staggering increase in the paper's circulation numbers, and on more than one occasion Daphne had overheard women – in queues for the bus, at a nearby table in a Lyons tea shop – chattering about her latest wisdom. She was, to put it mildly, a sensation. And pulling the plug on her simply was not an option. Halliday frowned and passed a careless hand over his thinning hair.

'Tell you what, you've caught me in a good mood, King. Fabian le Prince has caught some bug or another, probably ate some dodgy oysters at J. Sheekey's,' Halliday said, rising from his chair and turning to glance at the increasingly picturesque scene outside his window.

'So the culture desk's a man down. He was supposed to be paying a visit to Chester Harrison and his wife, Theodora what's-her-name, that French actress. From a few years back. Bit of a darling at one point. Made some godawful flicks though. Theodora D'Arby! Probably both before your time, King.'

Daphne raised her eyebrows in amusement. Theodora D'Arby was no more French than Fabian le Prince – or, to jettison his nom de plume, Frank Price. Theatre people, Daphne had always thought, with their predilection for ridiculous names and lofty pretensions, were to be approached with wariness.

'They're back in London to stage their great comeback, apparently. Been touring around all the usual spots – Reading, Scarborough, Blackpool – you name it. London's the final stop, the big hurrah,' Halliday went on. 'Course, the *Standard* have run their pot-stirring scrawlings about it already – courtesy of Tyrone Bridge. Apparently, the tour's not all gone . . . smoothly. A few ruffled feathers here and there. Bust-ups over bouquets, curtain-call fracas. Something about a narrow miss with a stage pulley. But le Prince was a shoo-in for a behind-the-scenes piece and now he's throwing up in bed rather than wining and dining in Shaftesbury Avenue. Not a scoop that'll win you a Pulitzer Prize, granted, but it's not . . . soufflés and begonias.' Halliday waved his hands haphazardly, as if fending off the advances of these womanly concerns. 'You'd be helping us out of a jam – le Prince was supposed to be at the Theatre Royale to meet D'Arby and Harrison in half an hour for a chinwag, then a nice little tour of the theatre – soak up the, uh, ambience. Plus of course front-row tickets for the show tonight. Game?'

Daphne cast a confused glance at Halliday. Was this a genuine offer? If she had known it would be this easy, she would have issued her subtle ultimatum before now. No extensive cajoling and campaigning required? To be presented with a gift horse was a rarity for Daphne; she must avert her eyes so as to avoid looking it in the mouth.

'Well, I . . . It's a bit tricky. I'm due to be catching the train this evening to see my mother and her lodger – I mean husband – in Slough. Then my older sister and her children are arriving the day after tomorrow – it'll be Christmas Eve after—'

Daphne caught herself: *What are you blathering about, you little fool?* Would Nellie Bly, pioneering journalist and Daphne's personal hero, have given her apologies because she had to hurry home to Mother? More to the point, would that unscrupulous rodent Jamie Jenkins? She pictured it now: this evening, with excessively milky tea, she would have to politely listen to Reg – former lodger, now stepfather – entertain himself and her mother with stories of japes at the book-ies, and reassure her mother that yes, she was perfectly content having a job, and no, she wouldn't be happier if she had a ring on her finger and a bun in the oven. On Christmas Eve Felicity would arrive with Daphne's nephew and nieces in tow, Tommy, Jenny and little Sarah. She hadn't had the chance to buy their Christmas presents yet; far too busy telling her readers how to stop their plum puddings from drying out or steering them through the challenges of cruel classmates telling their child that Father Christmas wasn't real.

No, she was resolved: a shorter trip to Slough this year. She would go tomorrow, allowing herself time to both grasp this unexpected opportunity and for a trip to Selfridges for the necessary gifts.

'Martin, kindly disregard those blatherings. Nothing would bring me greater pleasure than to go to London's West End on this most seasonal of days. Panto season seems to have passed me by this year, so a visit to the theatre won't go amiss.' Daphne gave one vigorous nod of her head. This was it, she had decided. Assertive, decisive, she would emerge from Dear Susan's shadow and show Martin that she, Daphne King, was a journal-ist to be reckoned with. 'You can count on me. After all, a King stepping in for a Prince, all very fitting.'

'There you are again, King – this poetry of yours is

just the ticket. Perhaps not one that'll get you on a direct line to the crime beat, but it's a ticket nonetheless. And mind you don't go getting any notions: you're still Dear Susan, but even she needs to stretch her legs – get out and about on the town every now and then.' Halliday rubbed his eyes and inhaled slowly. 'Now that's out of the way, be a doll and pop over to Luigi's to get me another bacon sandwich, would you? Feeling a bit ropey after all that mulled wine last night. Oh, and get yourself a copy of today's *Standard* – Tyrone Bridge's piece has a tasty bit of gossip about those two.'

For years afterwards, Daphne would revisit this moment in her mind. The moment when she decided to grasp an opportunity, however slight, to show her mettle. Perhaps she could join the culture desk permanently if she cut the mustard with this, give Dear Susan a send-off and allow her to rest in peace in the sweet hereafter. She would listen to some actors drone on about stage-craft, hear some mildly diverting anecdotes about dressing-room mishaps, then be on her way to endure Christmas with Mother and Reg.

And so it would have been for Daphne King.

Had it not, of course, been for the murder.

2

Daphne glided out of the *Chronicle*'s offices with all the cheer and optimism of a skater pirouetting on an ice rink. Usually, she would view such positivity with suspicion, treating it as a naive precursor to an unsightly tumble and an embarrassingly soggy aftermath. (To wit: her recent 'information sharing' exercise with that manipulative stoat, Jenkins.) However, she felt buoyed by a sense of purpose that had evaded her for some time now. The conversation with Martin Halliday had put an entirely new complexion on her day – on her vision of herself and her future. The telephone call to her mother had been brief and cheerful: she would, of course, be coming, but not today. Possibly tomorrow, possibly Christmas Eve. And she'd bring an extra bottle of sherry to make up for the delay.

Now, the snow swirling around her seemed to be embracing Daphne, propelling her forward. She purchased today's *Standard* from a vendor whose usual gruffness was currently juxtaposed with a lavish Father Christmas beard. In lieu of his traditional incoherent grunt by way of a thank you, he today proffered a jolly 'Deck the halls, ma'am!' to Daphne. Christmas really did have the queerest effect on people, she reflected.

Beneath the fragile shelter afforded by her umbrella (it had seen decidedly better days; she noted to herself that she must replace it in the January sales at Deben-hams) Daphne walked briskly to the bus stop. Her destination, the Theatre Royale, Great Windmill Street, lay but a mile or so away. The route of the number 24 bus would, Daphne calculated, allow her approximately twenty-four minutes during which to summon up the persona that she would present to Theodora D'Arby and her husband, Chester Harrison: that of a cultured sophis-ticate, accustomed to breakfasts at Claridge's, martinis at the Ritz and intellectual soirées in Bloomsbury.

Atop the bus, she conducted an inspection of her scuffed brown Oxford lace-ups (de rigueur according to the Littlewoods catalogue three years ago), the soggy knee-high socks which she preferred to stockings (these being far too prone to runs, and thus economically inef-ficient) and the pleated navy-blue skirt whose hem had defied numerous attempts at re-stitching. Daphne frowned. The sphere of theatrical types was fixated on appearances, that much she knew. Inhabiting the role of

Dear Susan required no superficial fripperies; utter anonymity was one benefit of having her work go unacknowledged. Her readers imagined Susan to be a moderately glamorous yet largely approachable housewife with an encyclopedic knowledge of the uses of bicarbonate of soda and the best strategies for combatting fungus gnats. Daphne and her socks could sit behind her typewriter and nobody was any the wiser. And even in her forays into off-the-record investigations, Daphne had found her slightly unkempt appearance an advantage. She doubted very much whether those women at that East End laundry would have been quite so forthcoming had she turned up with immaculate lipstick and a faultless coiffure.

Daphne King was entirely aware of the fact that she could lay no great claim to beauty, but her response to that was: rot. Sherlock Holmes certainly wasn't famed for being a looker, nor had he suffered because he wasn't *au courant* with fashion.

Abandoning her hasty sartorial inventory, Daphne turned her attention to a far more pressing matter: the copy of the *Standard* that she had stuffed into her satchel. Bypassing a headline proclaiming WOMAN FIGHTS BANDITS IN CINEMA AS MURDER DRAMA IS SCREENED (she would come back to that later) and several advertisements asking 'Are you struggling with crippling rheumatism?' (she hoped she would have no need of these for several decades yet), she flicked to the desired page and read on:

HARRISON AND D'ARBY RETURN TO THE WEST END
By Tyrone Bridge

With panto season well under way, cries of 'It's behind you!' echo along Shaftesbury Avenue. A fitting refrain as Chester Harrison and Theodora D'Arby trot back to London, tails between their legs – careers arguably well and truly behind them.

Those readers of a certain age may remember the duo from their 1919 production of *Hamlet*, in which Harrison directed D'Arby as the Dane. (This critic will, naturally, forgive any lapses in memory; in the sixteen years since D'Arby last deigned to tread the boards, many more memorable princes have contemplated this too, too sullied flesh.) Or perhaps readers will remember the pair's next theatrical coup, Harrison's self-penned *A Woman of Grace and Fury*, and the comparisons to Wilde and Shaw that were lavished upon it by critics less discerning than this one. Audiences lay prostrate at their feet, a golden couple with the Midas touch. A pity, some might say, that Hollywood was not so kind to the pair.

Hubris, ambition and, dare one say it, hints of a scandal whisked Harrison and D'Arby from our shores; failure and desperation have returned them here. Having toured the regional fleapits, Harrison now brings his production of *A Christmas Carol* to the capital, where we wait with bated breath to see his ragtag band of players make their West End debut tonight, 22nd December 1935. Regrettably, we are not yet to be granted the privilege of witnessing D'Arby grace our stage again, though this critic must profess that she would make a most convincing Ghost of Christmas Past.

Harrison and D'Arby may have once brought us a fine Prince of Denmark, but one's mind cannot help but alight upon two other Shakespearean figures now: King Lear, beseeching the universe to singe his white head as he roams the wilderness, and a self-aggrandising Bottom labouring under delusions of beauty.

Daphne raised her eyebrows and sighed. Vapid mutton dressed up as culturally scintillating lamb, she reflected. If one were to listen to Fleet Street tittle-tattle (which Daphne seemed compelled to do on occasion, but all in the name of professional expertise of course), one would know that Tyrone Bridge's standing as an excoriating reviewer had in recent years been superseded by his reputation as a mean-spirited little muckraker. And his Shakespearean references were bewilderingly haphazard: Daphne supposed that Chester Harrison was the decrepit, raving Lear, while Theodora D'Arby had been cast as Bottom in Bridge's confusing melange. The photograph accompanying the article (if one were generous enough to name it such; Daphne felt disinclined to) betrayed the inaccuracy of Tyrone Bridge's portrait, however. Daphne scrutinised the couple as they had been in 1919: Chester Harrison an extravagantly handsome man with an immaculate beard and a knowing smile upon his face, while Theodora's sphinx-like gaze and striking bob were mesmerising.

The bus hobbled along the Embankment, the glitteringly icy Thames to its south and thronging Christmas shoppers darting hither and thither towards Covent Garden. Daphne unscrewed her pen top and jotted down the one intriguing reference that she had chanced upon in Tyrone Bridge's otherwise anodyne ramblings: 'hubris, ambition and . . . scandal'. A potentially thrilling combination. There might be life in this story yet.

3

She hopped off the bus at Piccadilly Circus, where Eros was sporting a dazzling cloak of fresh snow. Some wag had also scaled the statue and delicately placed a somewhat limp Father Christmas hat atop the statue's head, lending him the faintly ridiculous air of a partygoer who had been abandoned by his pals. Snowflakes still giddily chivvying her along, Daphne headed in the direction of the Theatre Royale.

Approaching, she espied another figure making his way towards the theatre, the blue, red and yellow of his umbrella a defiant dash of colour against the white canvas of the metropolis. Once underneath the awnings, the man removed his gloves and stole a glance at the posters adorning the double doors: CHESTER HARRISON PRESENTS A CHRISTMAS CAROL. With his heavy yet slightly threadbare tweed coat pulled tight about him, a deep purple trilby hat and a raffish red scarf partly concealing his beard, the man appeared the embodiment of blithe bonhomie.

'Mr Harrison?' Daphne heard herself blurt. 'I say, Mr Harrison? Daphne King, *Chronicle*. How do you do?'

Daphne shook her umbrella a touch more vigorously than she had intended, treating Chester Harrison to a sprinkling of snow.

'Terribly sorry, Mr Harrison – damnably difficult to get this blasted thing down without a hellish furore. Do excuse me,' Daphne went on, inelegantly battling with her umbrella.

A grin that could only be described as devilish crept over Chester's face. 'Now, you strange creature, I've not the foggiest who you are – so far, you seem to have furnished me with a series of names, my own being foremost among them – but I'm rather taken with you already. Lamentably rare, a woman these days peppering her hellos with a "damnably", a "blasted" and a "hellish". More like the lingo one comes across in the pub after the dockers have knocked off.'

Daphne offered a distracted smile in response, her struggle to vanquish the umbrella ongoing. Despite the encumbrance, Daphne felt a new and queer boldness, a feeling that she, yes *she*, was entering a new arena. One in which boldness would be neither inappropriate nor queer to her.

'Alas, my talents were never appreciated in the ship-yards, but you'll find that the public houses of Fleet Street offer a similar lexical experience: colourful language and colourful characters, so they say. I'm from the *Daily Chronicle*. I know you were expecting Fabian le Prince, but he's been . . . Some regrettable business with oysters, I'm told,' Daphne explained, 'so you have me instead – and delighted I am to be here, too.'

With that, her umbrella finally succumbed to the surprising level of brute force that Daphne had been applying. She stuck out her hand to shake Chester's, but he brushed it aside, instead bestowing two continental kisses upon her cheeks.

'Oh yes! Of course. Theodora mentioned it at breakfast: a boon for us all, splashed across the pages of the *Chronicle*. What a treat. For my part, rather pleased to see the back of that le Prince chap. Always found him a touch too fawning. I suspect that you might be the sort that'll keep us all on our toes, Miss King,' he said merrily, bowing extravagantly as he did so. 'Oh and I insist upon your calling me Chester – only my accountant calls me Mr Harrison, and it sends a shiver down the spine somewhat.'

Daphne was on the point of uttering a witticism (something along the lines of it being *capital* to be there with such *assets* of English culture; she would *invest* in her writing, etcetera, etcetera) when her efforts at word-play were cut short by an interloper.

'You are fettered! Tell me why, spirit?' came a tremulously croaking voice.

'I wear the chain I forged in life,' recited Chester, spinning around with a flamboyant flourish. 'Although it's a trifle too tight around the neck now. Might ask the tailors to take it out a touch – what do you think?'

'Act One Scene Three has been, ahem, *finessed* to within an inch of its life. Any further tinkering from you, my dearest director, and I shall fear for *your* life.' A man, a mop of unkempt and wispy white hair swirling like a halo above his head, twinkling blue eyes glinting from a face etched with the lines and creases of age, gripped Chester firmly about the shoulders and embraced him warmly.

'Ebenezer Scrooge, I would expect nothing less than humbugs from you on this, our London press night.' Chester laughed and wagged a chastising finger.

Introductions were made. This was, it transpired, Robert Stirling or, as he had insisted on being called since being cast in the role of Scrooge, Ebbie. Robert had known Chester since their early music-hall days, auditioning for the same parts (and losing out to him) before Chester turned his hand to directing. For some thirty years, Robert had, with dogged and workmanlike dedication, built a sturdy, reliable career playing sturdy, reliable supporting roles: a reassuring second-in-command, a jolly uncle or, latterly, a genial great-uncle. Upon hearing the news that Chester and Theodora were returning not only to England but to the theatre with *A Christmas Carol*, Robert had campaigned tirelessly for the lead role.

Chester having made the necessary introductions, Robert delicately took Daphne's hand in his own and made to kiss it in the chivalric fashion. '*Enchanté*, as they say in gay Paree.'

'*Enchantée, monsieur*.' Daphne allowed herself the indulgence of an extravagant greeting. When in Rome and all that. '*Je suis ravie de parler avec vous tous et d'entendre parler de la production théâtrale*.'

Daphne had been *l'étoile* of her French class back in school; Madame Boucher always maintained that never had a student of hers been such a natural with the language, and Daphne had plunged head first into a love affair with all things French. Like all too many of the greatest affairs (so Daphne had read), it was torrid, unrequited and, for a spell, all-consuming. For the moment, however, blank looks were being exchanged between Chester and Robert.

'I'm afraid, my dear,' Chester declared with a winning smile, 'that your linguistic abilities exceed ours tenfold, if not thousandfold. The closest Robert has come to the Eiffel Tower is some overcooked steak and a carafe of cheap plonk at that brasserie around the cor—'

Robert cut in: 'While darling Chester has enjoyed one or two trips to Montmartre, but his French, ahem, *tongue* is only useful when whispering, *"Voulez vous cou—"'*

'Come come, Miss King,' Chester blurted, stifling a grin at Robert's jibe. 'I'm under strict orders from Theodora to show you some of our famous theatrical hospitality. Turn on the razzle-dazzle. I must advise you to have your thesaurus at the ready, poised to find innumerable synonyms for "brilliant", "bewitching" and "sublime". You can watch dear Robert here in his final rehearsal of a scene that's been proving infernally difficult to pin down.'

'Quite. Once more unto the breach, I say,' Robert proclaimed. 'Let's hope our Mr Hartforth has recovered from yesterday's tantrum. Surprised that he still has any toys left to throw out of his pram, the way he's been conducting himself.'

There was a momentary flicker of Chester's eyelashes before he turned to Daphne and explained: 'Mr Hartforth – Donald Hartforth – has a . . . shall we say . . . vexed relationship with suggestions about his acting. It might do to tread a little carefully around him. Rather bruised since an incident, a trifle really, in our Brighton stop on the tour; didn't take too kindly to some ideas from yours truly, saw fit to hurl a Christmas wreath at me.'

Robert laughed and then winced briefly, gripping his stomach, before tutting and rearranging the grimace, which was making a bid to overpower his easy smile. 'Pay no attention to me. Without being vulgar, I fear I'm being waylaid by a touch of dicky tummy. Wouldn't be surprised if it's gout – the blight of Henry VIII, myself and many other aged men with rather too much of a taste for red wine.'

'Hell's bells, Robert.' Chester directed a glance of concern at his friend. 'Something the matter?'

Robert waved a dismissive hand, straightening up while attempting unsuccessfully to conceal the effort that the movement required. 'No, no, nothing. This ghastly weather upsets my liver, that's all.'

'Spoken as Ebenezer himself would have it. Where the rest of the population is enjoying snowball fights and beguiled by a winter wonderland, you and your liver whinge about "ghastly weather".' Chester chuckled, his concern clearly not entirely dissipated. He had taken Daphne's left arm in his right, setting her hand gracefully upon the elbow of his coat.

An unassuming alleyway lay to the right of the ornate

main entrance to the theatre, and Daphne found herself ushered towards it, flanked by this pair of bon viveurs. She couldn't help but marvel at their sprightliness, both embodying a liveliness undimmed by advancing years. Daphne wondered whether she, when she came to be knocking on the door of sixty in the years to come, would be quite so puckish.

She suspected, though, that Chester's voluble confidence was laced with a touch of nervous trepidation about the evening's performance, and wondered whether Robert's easy charm, that of a man apparently content with his lot, similarly masked any press-night nerves – nerves perhaps manifesting themselves in the 'dicky tummy' he had spoken of so sheepishly.

What didn't, of course, occur to Daphne was that only one of the two men would set foot outside the theatre again.

4

'Run along now, Ebenezer. I'll see that Miss King here is fixed up with a glass of Christmas cheer and we'll see you directly.' Chester shooed Robert away as they passed through the stage door. After a righty-o and a gallant salute to the ludicrously tall man looming behind the desk that guarded the door, Robert trotted off along a corridor whose russet-red carpet was threadbare and whose walls were sprinkled with flaking white paint.

'Afternoon, Chester,' boomed the man at the desk. He had a large face, and the indecipherable expression upon it was rendered all the more puzzling by the bow tie adorned with grinning reindeer fixed about his neck.

'Ah, Nigel!' Chester exhaled. 'Miss King, please acquaint yourself with Mr Nigel Roberts, stalwart sentry of stage door. Nobody steps foot in our hallowed theatre without Nigel's say-so. Nigel, this is Miss King. She's our woman from the *Chronicle*, so do mind your p's and q's.' He winked at both Daphne and Nigel.

'Pleased to meet you, Nigel. And gosh, whatever you do, please don't mind any p's on my account – let your p's remain liberated, and certainly no hemming-in of those q's either,' Daphne burbled brightly. 'Of all the citizens of the alphabet, they really are the ones you oughtn't to rein in.'

'You'll find us a rum lot, Miss King, especially these two old dogs.' Nigel's words were convivial but, Daphne noted, he seemed to have forgotten to notify his face that a smile was required.

'Speaking of rum, I'll whisk you to the bar, then we'll to the stage to see what's what with this scene. We have gin, wine, brandy – and possibly champagne, if Robert hasn't drained us dry.' Chester was revelling in the role of host, and he clapped his hands together crisply to signal that they ought to be on their way.

'Oh, before you go, Chester, another parcel arrived for you today,' Nigel said. 'Peculiar, it is. Same as yesterday, looks to be.'

Was that a flicker of dread that crossed Chester's face? Did Daphne detect a suggestion of . . . panic in his eyes? Chester cleared his throat, and when he spoke, it was quietly, tersely. Daphne was startled by the shift from his previously gregarious, jesting tone.

'Thank you, Nigel. Your assistance, as ever, is appreciated. As is your discretion. Leave it in the usual place, please.'

A moment passed during which Daphne considered enquiring about this parcel, but her instincts told her that the judicious moment was not now. Chester's smile reappeared – though, Daphne fancied, with less certainty than before – and he began navigating them along the corridors, explaining the genius that lay in casting only four actors to bring *A Christmas Carol* to life. Daphne would meet them in due course, he assured her, and they would all be entirely at her disposal.

As they made countless left and right turns through the backstage warren, Daphne began to feel that they were wending their way through an ants' nest or a beehive; through sites of industry towards a pulsating centre. The atmosphere became purposeful yet frenzied, the narrow corridors alive with activity. They passed a pair of burly stagehands arguing who had been at fault in chipping a coffin mid-hoist; Daphne excused herself after bumping into a wardrobe assistant whose face was sodden with tears and whose garbled wailings suggested that she had ironed a hole in Bob Cratchit's trousers.

Daphne was then startled to realise that Chester had embarked upon a monologue of unprompted candour. He knew, he was intoning, that this time tomorrow his fate would be sealed. When he and Theodora had abandoned London in favour of America some sixteen years ago, he had burned too many bridges, disappointed too many friends and colleagues. He had been setting the West End alight: his *Twelfth Night* a popular crowd-pleaser, audiences rolling in the aisles during *The Importance of Being Earnest*. By the time *A Woman of Grace and Fury* made its debut, he could do no wrong: 'Midas' Harrison's golden touch left critics swooning and box offices under siege. In the eyes of many, he had forsaken all of this at the whim of an impetuous woman twenty years his junior. Hollywood had for Chester been an idle interlude during which his ambition had numbed and his talents lay dormant. Theodora's career had taken precedence, but it transpired they had backed the wrong horse – though of course he would never say such a thing to Theodora directly. Now, here they were, accomplishments tinged with nostalgia and melancholy, and the future uncertain, although Chester was sure that, by returning to England and proving his talents once more, his reputation would be resurrected. At the Theatre Royale the stage was set for him to play the role of theatrical impresario once more.

'Stirring stuff, eh, Miss King?' He twinkled at her.

Chester, now rumbling in a baritone at once jaunty and authoritative about theatre being the beating heart of London, explained his casting choices. His staging of *A Christmas Carol* adopted the fashionable *soi-disant* minimalistic approach that was all the go on the continent. Not for him the management of scores of bit-part players and the balancing of dozens of oppositional egos. No, a cast of four actors sufficed to bring Dickens' story to life, four, Chester reflected, being *quite* enough to keep one occupied. Robert, of course, giving his all to Scrooge. Then there was Donald Hartforth, whose, ahem, magnetism seemed to have quadrupled in intensity since having been cast in four roles: Jacob Marley *and* all the ghosts – of Christmases Past, Present and Yet to Come. And of course Irene Juniper. Her incarnation of Tiny Tim did, one had to admit, tug at the heartstrings. And finally there was, blessedly, the unassuming Cecil Milford, whose Bob Cratchit was all the more beguiling for Cecil's apparent lack of artifice.

Daphne was rather bamboozled by this list of names and epithets, and later would wish that she had paid a little more attention to Chester's descriptions. Might they have given an inkling of what was to come? No matter. Chester now opened a door that led them into the auditorium proper, and Daphne followed, self-consciously glancing at the puddles she had realised she was leaving behind her on the carpet.

In the middle of the stage were two figures. The woman's auburn ringlets bounced about her shoulders as she paced back and forth, and, despite her diminutive stature, her presence was a formidable one. The man, on the other hand, affected a posture of easy nonchalance, a cigarette dangling from his lips. His protruding ears (rather becoming), pencil moustache (perfectly trim) and jet-black hair sculpted sharply in a faultless side parting called to mind Clark Gable.

'I told you, Donald – I've told them as well – I am *not* staying here if *he* is!' the woman spat, the venom in her words evident.

'Sweetie, Irene darling,' purred the man, 'it won't be much longer, I promise. I said I'll fix it.'

Daphne had caught up with Chester and glanced at him. Just as earlier, when Nigel on the stage door had made mention of parcels, Chester's face was now stony. He took a deep breath, seemed to recall that he was not alone, then constructed an expression of bemused exasperation.

'Come come, little ones, darling Donald, Irene my sweet,' he cooed to the pair onstage as he approached at considerable speed. 'We've rehearsing to be getting on with, and rather urgent rehearsing at that. So let's leave whatever little to-do you're discussing behind us.'

The woman snorted, fixing a contemptuous glare upon him. 'A plague on the lot of you.' She charged off the stage, leaving the man behind her.

Chester made no attempt to elucidate whatever was the matter, but merely clapped his hands and declared, 'Act One Scene Three. If you please, Donald.'

Onstage, Donald Hartforth exhaled deeply. Carelessly flicking his cigarette to the boards, he smoothed his thin moustache with the long index finger of his left hand. 'Bugger of a thing, Chester, but funnily enough we do need your beloved Robert here for that scene. Unless you've finally decided to cut the old buffer loose?'

Chester patiently replied, 'Robert will be here momentarily, Donald. Perhaps you could utilise this interlude to . . . limber up, as they say?'

He turned to Daphne and, with an eye roll that seemed tinged with something resembling desperation, whispered confidingly, 'Actors. Can't live with 'em, can't live without 'em. As tempting as it is to attempt the latter, on occasion.'

Donald's swaggering Gable-esque demeanour gave way to the role he was to inhabit for this scene: that of the Ghost of Christmas Past. His matinee idol features contorted as he set about conjuring an otherworldly sprite, puckering his mouth into an insolent grimace.

Chester, whispering again, told Daphne, 'Of course, he'll be in black shrouds for this, and we've some newfangled device that'll make him seem like he's levitating. Modern theatrics, dontcha know.'

Donald clambered around the array of gravestones which littered the stage, his physicality bespeaking an infernal creature, limbs jolting and grimace steady and gleeful.

'That's super, Donald,' Chester declared. 'That's it, nail on the head. After all, you're not Ariel, floating about on a desert island, you're a dark spirit dragged from the underworld to awaken mankind to their sins and regrets.'

Donald rolled his eyes perceptibly at this before standing upright and replying, 'A patronising pat on the back is all well and good, but where the bloody hell's Robert? I can't go on gurning indefinitely, you know.'

At that, Robert made his entrance on to the stage. His steps were oddly tentative, as though he were still picking his way through the snow outside. He made his way through the gravestones, leaning on one and grasping his side.

Daphne frowned and squinted. Chester cleared his throat again and turned to her. 'We've always played this scene too safe, too sanitised; it's Scrooge on the point of being shown his own grave, for Christ's sake. We want the audience to *feel* it.'

Daphne was certainly feeling something. Not thrilled, not riveted, but rather a growing sense that all was not as it should be.

Robert was now swaying back and forth, and he emitted a sound – a slurred line perhaps? His head swivelled towards Chester and Daphne to reveal glassy eyes and a face slick with sweat.

'Chester, I think something's wrong,' Daphne uttered in not quite a whisper. 'He looks really rather ill.'

'Magic of make-up, my dear, magic of make-up,' Chester hushed her.

Donald stopped his clambering and stared at Robert quizzically.

'It's your line, Robert: "Assure me that I yet may change these shadows you have shown me, by an altered life." Really, Chester, am I to do everything around here?' Donald exclaimed as he turned to his director, casting about for assistance in chivvying his co-star into action.

A groan escaped from Robert's mouth, which was fixed in a grimace. His eyes were rolling wildly, his arms outstretched and shaking.

Robert staggered one awful step further.

His final step.

As if detaching from his swaying body, Robert's head lolled about, finally jolting to face Chester. A flash of lucidity momentarily streaked across his eyes, before it turned to fear.

Then, a sickening thud as Robert crashed to the floor.

5

Daphne bolted towards the stage. She experienced the queer sensation of being filled with a sense of urgency, the imperative to action, but knowing herself to be utterly impotent. Something within her screamed that it was already too late: that Robert hadn't merely slipped into unconsciousness. That he was dead. Though her eyes were fixed on Robert's inert form slumped in front of a gravestone, she was aware of the incongruity of the plump ornamental cherubs perched on the proscenium, peering down at the macabre scene below.

Surprised at her own agility, Daphne hoisted herself up onto the stage and scrambled towards Robert.

In years to come, when Daphne recalled this moment, it was his eyes that caused her to shiver. Had they been voids, empty of awareness and lucidity, that would have been far preferable to the cruel truth: his eyes were shot through with pain, fear, desperation.

Rolling back Robert's sleeve, she checked his wrist

for a pulse. Nothing. His neck was similarly still. Nothing.

It is often said that *in extremis* events appear to happen in slow motion. Survivors of automobile accidents attest to feeling that their vehicles moved at a sluggish pace in a lethargic world during collisions that in reality only lasted two or three seconds; life-altering mishaps occurring ponderously, as if testing whether the universe is equipped to manage their ramifications while they watched impotently.

Daphne, on the other hand, discovered that she was able to manage the moment. She had not even been conscious of dropping to her knees to check for Robert's pulse, so automatic a reflex had it been. She now straightened up and surveyed the scene: the man who had before been so sinuously intimidating as the Ghost of Christmas Past now stood stock still, staring blankly at Robert's fallen body. That, at least, was Daphne's first impression, before she realised that Donald was, in fact, staring at her. As if unperturbed by Robert's lifeless body, and more concerned about her presence – or what she was going to do.

Chester, meanwhile, was still down in the stalls, bewilderment flooding his face. He clutched his beard, one step away from outright gnashing his teeth. Croaky and feeble, the voice emanating from him struck a note of incongruity, lacking as it did any correlation with his solidly built figure.

He stuttered, 'Is h-he . . . is Robert . . .?'

He seemed unable to speak the word.

'He's dead, yes. I'm quite certain,' Daphne stated calmly. 'And right now we need to cover the poor man up and fetch the police.'

Turning to Donald, Daphne resisted the impulse to tell him to pull himself together and do something; instead, she coolly instructed him to bring her his black shroud and then to alert the authorities. By her reckoning, Inspector Marklow and his bobby would most likely be enjoying a break in the Soho bun shop they favoured around this hour every day. Donald was to make his way there – a three-minute trot which would bring the police far more speedily than a telephone call. His gills distinctly green, Donald shuffled forward and – without coming any closer than strictly necessary – flung his shroud towards Daphne before fleeing from the stage. *Artistic types are so damned queasy*, Daphne thought to herself.

She was aware of a noise emanating from Chester, part wail, part whimper. Entirely unintelligible. She was also aware that she ought to go and comfort the old man. His friend had died before his eyes, and here he was, alone with a stranger. The least she could do was offer him a sturdy arm around the shoulders. However, surrounded by gravestones, a dead body before her, Daphne King felt a remarkable stillness. A clarity of purpose which allowed no room for comforting Chester Harrison. Her nerves were not jangling, her mind was crystal clear. Only one sentiment pulsed within her cranium, a sentiment that would come to nudge at her intermittently over the course of the next two days: *Something was wrong and she needed to find out what it was.*

Chester was making his way haltingly up onto the stage, his whimpering now a disconcertingly soft muttering. Daphne knew she hadn't long to make her assessment of the scene. As she was arranging the shroud over Robert's inert corpse, she was struck by two things. Firstly, some greyish liquid in the corner of Robert's mouth. It seemed indecent to note the smear, something curiously intimate about it. But Daphne cared not two straws for decency at that moment. Secondly, some smudges, a vibrant orange colour, beside his breast pocket. She was certain they hadn't been there when she had met Robert earlier. A feeling was beginning to tickle at her insides; a feeling she would learn not to ignore.

Silence and inertia overtook the stage. How many minutes had passed? Five? Perhaps ten? Suddenly, Chester let out a sharp stab of a cry, tears springing to his eyes. 'I might have done something. Why did I have to be so pig-headed? So stuck on my own . . . What have I done?'

What *had* he done, Daphne was on the point of asking, when she was interrupted by the arrival of the police.

6

'Well I'll be . . .' a rotund figure exclaimed, briskly striding towards Daphne while depositing the last of an iced bun in his mouth. 'Miss King! What a pleasure to see you again. Bet you've been having a whale of a time – another death to get those cogs of yours whirring over!'

There wasn't an ounce of ill-will in his remarks; Inspector Marklow was a man for whom sarcasm or irony were foreign beasts to be avoided for one's own safety. He was incapable of facade or artifice; his utter inability to deploy tact, sugar the pill or concoct half-truths was a trait which, while perhaps arguably noble in a layman, did not sit well with the business of outwitting criminals and interpreting nuances in behaviour. The man said what he thought, thought what he saw, consequences and subtleties be damned. Unfortunately for the inspector, this trait meant that he was prone to telling witnesses that their testimonies were bunkum or immediately revealing his suspicions to potential culprits, thereby affording them the opportunity to dispose of any evidence or sew up any holes in their alibis. Fortunately for Daphne, on the other hand, it meant that he had no qualms about sharing morsels of information with her over a cup of tea.

They had met eighteen months ago, when Daphne had gone to Scotland Yard with her dossier of evidence about the Gambling Contessa, and since then they had developed an easy (and for Daphne professionally beneficial) friendship. Daphne had even been invited to the christening of Marklow's son last month.

'Indeed, Inspector Marklow,' she replied. 'Though I ought to say that I take no joy from the death of poor Mr Stirling. This is Mr Chester Harrison, it seems a dear friend of the deceased.'

At this Chester's strength appeared to give way. Daphne quickly grasped his arms, supporting him.

'Quite, quite.' Marklow cleared his throat. 'My condolences. From what this fellow told me on our way from the bun shop –' he gestured to Donald '– it sounds like a straightforward case of a dicky heart – very often the way with these elderly gents. I'll have a look, but dare say I'll be home by teatime.' He glanced at his wristwatch. 'Last day before I'm on my holidays; little Johnny's first Christmas, you see. Nessa'll have my guts for garters if I'm home late tonight – doing sherry and mince pies with the neighbours – so let's hop to it.'

Daphne frowned. Straightforward case of a dicky heart? Exactly what had Donald Hartforth told Marklow? Her experience of Marklow's investigation methods told her that he was all too ready to accept at face value any testimony slung his way. Although Daphne would deny it to the hilt, she couldn't quite suppress the feeling of excitement that was bubbling within her. Halliday had sent her here to pen a frivolous puff piece, but here she was, yards from a dead body, with suspicions tantalisingly close to crystallising in her mind.

Marklow explained that he and the nervous-looking young officer beside him would need to conduct a preliminary examination of the corpse, but before they did so he sidled over to Daphne and whispered, 'Anyone famous in this? Nessa would bite her left arm off to get an autograph from a star.'

7

Neither Chester nor Donald seemed capable of doing anything useful. The former was now glassy-eyed with shock, the latter apparently dumbstruck and witless. Daphne, therefore, derived no small amount of furtive pleasure in taking the bull by the horns (she could hear Madame Boucher now, declaring, '*Daphne, il faut, comment dit-on* . . . take the bull by the horns!') and giving instructions to both men. Slowly, clearly and calmly, she explained that she would escort Chester to the bar in the foyer of the theatre, while Donald was to gather the actors and any other members of the company and bring them along too. She couldn't help but feel that this troupe of bohemians might benefit from glasses of hot brandy and water to steady them, judging from the catatonic reactions of Chester and Donald.

Decisions made, instructions issued, Daphne felt carried along by a surge of something akin to elation. Already she felt herself uprooting the simpering wallflower so often trodden upon at the offices of the *Chronicle*, planting in its stead a sturdy, unyielding oak. A sapling maybe, but an oak nonetheless.

Having deposited a visibly trembling Chester at the bar, Daphne had a telephone call to make. She made her way to the stage door, offered a brief explanation of events to Nigel, ever-vigilant keeper of the door and its facilities, and dialled the number of the *Chronicle*.

'What the bloody hell's going on over there, King? I've heard on the grapevine that some old duffer's snuffed it? Leaves us a bit high and dry, doesn't it. Couldn't he have waited till after opening night to meet his maker? We'll have to fill the empty slot with . . . I don't know . . . Dear Susan's top tips for mistletoe arrangements?'

Ah. Martin Halliday's famous sympathy for human tragedy. And Martin Halliday's famous grapevine – a network of loose-lipped constables at Scotland Yard whose willingness to share information at lightning speed was both alarming and impressive. Daphne barely suppressed an arch smile; she would not have bothered to suppress it at all, were it not for the presence of the watchful Nigel.

'The thing is, Martin, I've a notion that we won't need to fill the pages,' she began slowly, weighing each word carefully. If she gave away too much too soon, Halliday would insist that Jamie Jenkins be parachuted in to scoop up the scandal. If, on the other hand, she withheld too much, Halliday would turn his nose up at the story. It was a perilous tightrope to navigate. 'You see, I've a notion that this could be . . . *something*.'

A pause, during which she could hear Martin Halliday's offputtingly heavy breathing.

'*Something*? You think this could be *something*?' His voice wavered between irritation and boredom. 'Have I missed anything here, Daphne?'

'You quite possibly have. And perhaps I have, so far. But I can assure you that I won't be missing anything else. I think I ought to stay here and get to the bottom of whatever there is . . . to get to the bottom of.'

Seemingly taken aback by the unmistakably tart undertone to Daphne's response, Martin paused, then sighed in exasperation. 'King, you . . . I'm not sure I follow. You're going to have to give me more.'

Daphne glanced up at Nigel, whose arms were folded as he stared at the door to the alley, apparently transfixed by it. She shifted slightly, turning and lowering her voice.

'I can't right now, so you're just going to have to trust me. I can smell something, Martin. Something that's not quite right. If there's something to write about, surely you want it to be the *Chronicle* that writes about it. A man died, yes, but I think there's more to it. I was right about the Gambling Contessa, wasn't I? And if the *Standard* gets a whiff of something and you've already pulled me out of here – well, I can't see that going down well, can you?'

When in doubt, Daphne knew, it was best to appeal to Martin's desire to get one over on their rivals.

He exhaled deeply. 'Fine, King. Fine. You're already there; you're our woman on the inside. Stick to them all like glue. Sniff out whatever it is. Ferret it out of them. At the very least, I want tears, tantrums, I want to know what the old codger's last bleedin' words were, his dying declaration.'

'Yes sir, Mr Halliday. Roger that. I will endeavour to deliver you an early Christmas present of sensation and scandal.' Daphne flinched slightly at her own enthusiasm. All she had so far was a dead old man and a distinct feeling in her waters. All of which could disappointingly amount to a proverbial lump of coal. No matter. Daphne felt invigorated, the thrill of the story ahead of her. Assuring him that she wouldn't let him down, Daphne slammed the telephone back into the receiver.

'Thank you, Nigel, I'll leave you in peace now,' she chirped merrily as she turned to leave. A thought struck her, however, and stopped her abruptly.

'Nigel, I . . . I don't suppose you need me to take

anything up for Chester? Any of those . . . parcels?' she asked, congratulating herself on both her quick thinking and her performance of guileless naivety.

'Very kind of you, Miss King,' Nigel answered. 'But Chester asked for any more parcels to be brought directly up to his dressing room, put with the others.'

'Oh I see, jolly good. Exactly how many have there been, Nigel?'

'Let's see. The company arrived here, what, five days ago? Yes, last Thursday, and I'd say there's been one a day, so, let's see, that'd be . . . five. Yes, all in all, I'd estimate that there's been five.'

Daphne frowned at the laboured arithmetic and its conclusion: one parcel every day for Chester was perhaps not all that curious. He was, after all, a famed theatre director arriving back in London with not a little fanfare. What was curious, however, was Chester's response earlier to Nigel's announcement about another one. To be addressed later, Daphne decided. Immediate priorities recalled themselves to her. There would be no dithering, no trifling; the story would be hers, and hers alone.

It was here, however, that Daphne's mind, moments earlier so poised, became a maelstrom of conflicting impulses. She was an interloper here: she had no personal attachment to anyone under the Theatre Royale's roof, so could claim no sentimental reason to explain her presence, but nor was she, strictly speaking, here on a professional venture any longer. Her initial objective – to pen a pleasingly complimentary and inoffensive puff piece designed to lure the punters to Shaftesbury Avenue – had been derailed by the death of a cast member. And not just any cast member: Scrooge himself. Daphne was in a precarious position. What was to prevent Chester, or indeed anyone else, from politely asking her to vacate the premises? Why on earth should they allow a perfect stranger to remain present at such a catastrophic juncture?

Making through the labyrinthine corridors, Daphne removed her glasses to clean them and adjusted her satchel on her shoulder. She let out a sigh. She had two options: she could go and introduce herself to the rest of the company, no doubt to bafflement as to her continued presence, or she could make herself useful by finding that something illustrated her value.

Robert's dressing room it was. Before Marklow and his sidekick beat her to it.

8

Lest she be intercepted, Daphne scuttled with all her stealth along the corridor lined with dressing-room doors. Although she could overhear muffled conversations going on in almost every room, and the temptation to eavesdrop exerted a nearly irresistible pull, Daphne was determined not to be swayed from her mission: to reach Robert's dressing room while it was still untouched by the police.

Mercifully, the doors were adorned with name plates, and she spotted Robert's at the end of the corridor. Inside, his coat was still upon its hook, a tattered script lying on the table before a mirror. Daphne was taken aback by how cluttered the room was, but not with theatrical paraphernalia, make-up or anything that suggested the glamour of an actor's life. No, Robert Stirling's dressing room resembled the rather squalid bedroom of a particularly slovenly bachelor. Empty wine glasses were scattered carelessly about the place, while here was a rogue sock, there a stained cup.

Daphne screwed up her nose. The company had only been in residence for five days and this was the state of the room already. Robert had seemed dapper and well turned out, not slatternly and slipshod. First impressions, Daphne reflected, really could be deceiving.

She scanned the room for anything of interest, but found only the remains of various foodstuffs: a few discarded pigs-in-blankets on a greasy plate, a rather hefty slice of Christmas cake already acquiring an unbecoming fringe of mould. Her eyes alighted on the remnants of some sandwiches, crusts partially nibbled and fillings left untouched. Messy *and* wasteful, Robert had turned out to be. Although, she reflected, there did appear to be rather a lot of fried mushrooms in the sandwiches, so perhaps one couldn't blame him entirely for leaving them.

A penny began to clatter in Daphne's mind. Not quite dropping yet, but teetering. Hadn't Robert had stomach trouble earlier that day? Daphne prodded at the mushrooms, examining them carefully. One of the benefits of being Dear Susan was her nigh-on encyclopedic knowledge of England's flora – the pests that beset them, the propagation methods that suited them.

Her research into botany and horticulture had taken her on some intriguing detours, one of which had led her to delve into the world of poisonous mushrooms. And in Robert's sandwiches, as plain as the nose on her face, as clear as day is day and night is night, lay a particularly savage variety of poisonous mushroom: *Amanita virosa* or, in common English, destroying angel.

9

Like every other room in the Theatre Royale, the bar was something of a palimpsest. Despite the watermarks on the shabby walnut tables, the frayed – and in places missing – tassels on the red lampshades and the ripped and worn leather on the bar stools, one could still conjure up the grandeur and opulence of the theatre as it had been when first built, when the glow of the lampshades would have called to mind the sophistication of a Left Bank salon. The walls were scattered with dozens of framed photos of former productions: here, a Cleopatra clasped a serpent to her bosom; there, two dapper gentlemen were captured mid-air, grins on their faces, tap shoes upon their feet. In the corner was propped a Christmas tree which had already been abandoned by most of its needles. It peered with unmistakable melancholy over the group which had assembled itself.

Daphne observed the unmerry band, whose members were making only the most cursory gestures towards conversation. There were five of them: Donald Hartforth of course, two younger men she had not seen before and the ringleted, enraged petite woman who had stormed off the stage earlier. The fifth and evidently the most unmerry of them all was Chester. Slumped in a chair in the corner, a slight tremor in the hand which held a black cup, he showed little sign of being aware of his surroundings and companions. Of the convivial and sanguine host who had greeted Daphne earlier, there was little sign.

Holding forth was Donald Hartforth. He presided with bombast, one brown brogue perched on a crate of empty bottles, the other planted squarely on the floor. Another cigarette was hanging from beneath his moustache, and with his hands he was shaping and carving the air around him. To his admirers, a dedicated coterie who had followed his career with an evangelical fervour, these gestures had the elegant potency of a conductor at the helm of the London Philharmonic, the swooping beauty of a murmuration of starlings. To those less taken by the man's flourishes (the critics at *Stage Bugle* or *Theatre Today*, to name but two), the incessant swishing was yet more proof of the man's questionable command of the acting profession. Donald Hartforth was a divisive figure in London's Theatreland. His ability to generate both rapture and derision, ticket sales and pithily snooty headlines, was the primary reason behind Chester's casting of him. Setting tongues wagging and getting derrières on seats were Hartforth specialities.

The ringleted young woman was lying on her back a few yards from Donald's feet. Raising alternate legs with rhythmic regularity, she was emitting a slow steady breath with each movement and listening attentively as Donald continued with his monologue.

'Well, I'll say this for Robert: he never let his lack of talent get in the way of his career. Even a *butcher's* lad could have handled verse with more delicacy than *Robert*. Left the Bard positively *eviscerated*. Hung, drawn and *quartered*.' Donald's words were catapulted forth with a gleeful mixture of cruelty and relish. He raised the glass of red wine in his left hand. 'Exit stage left, Robert, pursued by a mediocre legacy.'

'Hear, hear,' began the woman from her prostrate position. 'Out with the lascivious old lech, the clunking old ham; in with the dashing new piece of prime sirloin steak. You of course, Donald,' she concluded parenthetically.

Donald brought a hand to his brow, a gesture intended to suggest humility, but which in fact served the purpose of confirming that his heavily pomaded black hair remained fixed in place. 'Oh Irene, my filet *mignon*, you do *spoil* me,' he drawled, now swirling his left hand in an exaggerated bow before taking an elegant drag upon his cigarette.

Well, well, Daphne thought, *what do we have here?* A malevolent duo spewing forth some rather intriguing titbits. It felt almost cruel to remain unannounced in the doorway, allowing them to continue, unaware of her presence.

Too late, however, for Chester returned abruptly from his reverie. Attempting to lift himself out of his arm-chair, he croaked weakly, 'Ah, Miss King, I see you're still here.'

She took a deep breath.

'Yes, I . . . I've been here since we . . . since, that is to say, I've been here since Robert died,' she managed uncertainly, all eyes in the bar suddenly upon her. 'I'm afraid I have some news, something that might prove troubling.'

'Forgive me –' Donald squinted slightly, his foot still on the crate '– but precisely who *are* you?'

'Ah yes, of course. We met under rather inauspicious circumstances earlier. Do allow me to introduce myself: Daphne King – from the *Chronicle*. Here to do a little behind-the-scenes puff piece,' she said, keen to dispose of the niceties so that she could get to the meat of her announcement. 'As I was saying, I have something that I think bears —'

'How do you do, Miss King.' He shook her hand firmly. 'I'm Donald Hartforth.'

'Yes, I know who you—'

Daphne's attempt to interject was flatly ignored, as Donald continued: 'I'm playing all the ghouls in the play: ghosts of past, present and yet to come, as well as jolly old Jacob Marley. I'm also renowned as a charming leading man, a charismatic Shakespearean actor and future matinee idol of the moving pictures.' An exaggerated batting of his eyelids concluded his introduction.

Recollecting Donald Hartforth's inability to move or speak when Robert had keeled over, Daphne noted that he had forgotten to mention the other role he had played to perfection less than an hour ago: that of the unspeakably useless bystander in a time of crisis. She attempted to arrange a warm if insouciant smile upon her face, while Donald fixed her with an even stare, and his companion – she of the floor exercises – stood up.

Irene Juniper viewed Daphne with the curiosity displayed by visitors to a primate enclosure or spectators at a circus sideshow. As a member of the Ladies' League of Health and Beauty, an organisation dedicated to, as their monthly magazine stated, 'feminine radiance and corporeal suppleness – for ladies who don't want to bulge where they oughtn't to', Irene possessed an almost evangelical belief in the importance of keeping up appearances. Her fellows at the League would have rolled their sleeves up (delicately, of course, being sure not to crease their satin blouses) and transformed this dishevelled and disordered specimen into a beacon of feminine radiance. Perhaps Irene could take her under her wing, nurture this poor creature, sew that hem up. But Irene dismissed such trifling thoughts immediately; she had her career to think about – her star was on the rise, she was certain of it – and taking on woebegone types such as this was an altruistic step too far. She wasn't a philanthropist, after all.

'How lovely to have you here, Miss King. I suppose you must be rather nervous, meeting a pack of West End legends. But don't worry; we may not look it, but we *are* all human, I assure you.' Irene spoke slowly, as if addressing an elderly great-aunt whose hearing was failing and whose marbles were long gone.

Daphne smiled and removed her glasses, which had begun to steam up again. 'That's very kind of you. Forgive me, but I really must tell you all what I've—'

At this, Irene's generosity of spirit faltered, evidently galled at not even being asked her name. 'I'm Irene Juniper, Miss King. Perhaps you saw me last year in *All Girls Go to Heaven*? Or you might have caught *The Maid of Montmartre* the year before?' Daphne's affably blank face answered Irene's questions. 'I see. Not a theatre-goer, Miss King?'

'Guilty as charged, Miss Juniper. More of a cinema gal, all said. More likely to be at the Coronet than at the Haymarket, I'm afraid,' Daphne replied. 'Did you see *Little Women*? Hepburn was a knockout, truly a knockout.'

Irene responded with a wan smile before commencing windmill motions, her arms rotating with alarming velocity. This prompted a guffaw from Donald. He had known Irene for several years, sharing as they did the same agent; consequently, he was entirely familiar with just how querulous she could become when confronted with the unthinkable – a member of the public ignorant of her artistic output.

'As I was saying,' Daphne attempted once more, 'there's something—'

'Miss King, we can't have you standing there like a lemon without a drink in hand.' The Chester of old seemed to be making a reappearance. 'Rarely was Robert seen without one, so we must honour his memory.'

At that, he winked at the young man who had installed himself behind the bar.

'Yes, I'll be mother!' the young man exclaimed, before zigzagging towards Daphne brandishing a bottle of wine and a glass. There was an excitable affability about him as he vigorously shook Daphne's hand. His shirt sleeves rolled up to his elbows, dabs of grey paint visible on his black trousers, he introduced himself as Alfred Burford, assistant stage manager – a role he had taken on after finishing art school in the summer of last year. With his unruly mop of tousled brown hair and a gap between his front teeth, Alfred seemed at once guileless and inquisitive, an eager schoolboy presenting his jotter to a teacher for approval.

'Helluva thing, isn't it, Miss King – Robert's death,' Alfred said in a distractingly buoyant tone as he rolled on the balls of his feet. 'He rubbed people up the wrong way, but he wasn't all bad.'

'I wouldn't be quite so sure of that, Alfred,' Irene Juniper muttered as she attended to some ringlets displaced during her exertions.

Chester, ignoring Irene's remark, continued with his introductions. 'And this is Cecil Milford. Won't find a keener boyo in all of Shaftesbury Avenue, if you ask me,' he announced with pride.

Alfred, having safely installed a glass of wine in Daphne's hand, was now nodding along, one foot swinging back and forth, as though waging a never-ending battle against the encroaching forces of stillness. In contrast to Alfred's jittering, Cecil Milford, the man next to him, was an island of tranquillity. His face transmitting benevolence, he possessed an almost bovine docility that was amplified by his extravagantly long eyelashes. His hair preternaturally golden, his eyes a cerulean blue, dimples in unblemished alabaster cheeks, he resembled a Greek god made flesh. One who had been cast out from Mount Olympus as punishment for being absurdly handsome.

'Yes, mustn't forget dear old Cecil.' Alfred was beaming now, and clapped the man on the back. 'He's our Bob Cratchit.'

Cecil blushed at the sudden turning of the spotlight upon him and mumbled something about being lucky to be there. *Of course*, Daphne thought, *Bob Cratchit, the literary embodiment of human decency, kindness and humility*. Such qualities radiated from the eyes of Cecil Milford, though Daphne wondered whether Dickens had imagined his Cratchit to be such a dish.

Daphne glanced at the dangerously full glass of red wine in her left hand and around at the theatre folk around her and realised that she had failed to string together one coherent sentence since entering the bar. If she were to crack this case and get her name on the *Chronicle*'s front page, she really would need to pull her socks up. She couldn't let the wallflower's tendrils take hold again. She had stated her case assertively and plainly to Martin Halliday on the telephone, a feat in itself, and if she could muster the courage to argue her cause to the man who had relegated her to the sidelines for years, she could bloody well knock a few sentences together for this band of thespians.

Placing her glass on the nearest table, she prepared to launch into her revelation.

10

'Ah, here you all are,' came Marklow's voice from the doorway. 'Right, well, far as we can see it, old fella's heart gave out. Not a scratch on him, looks as peaceful as I'd like to be when I go to meet my maker. Boys at the mortuary will have a closer look; we just need to ask you all a few questions.'

'Inspector, if I might be so bold as to—' Daphne said, only for Marklow to throw an uncharacteristically sharp glance at her.

'Be as bold as you like, King, but once I've clocked off, if you please. It's half past three now; my shift's over in half an hour.'

There followed an interlude during which Marklow made his way around those gathered, posing the same three questions to each of them. When did you last see the deceased? Where were you this afternoon and evening? What was your relationship to the deceased?

The anodyne responses appeared to bore the inspector,

who made no attempt to stifle his yawns. All, it tran-spired, had seen Robert that very afternoon, and none could offer anything noteworthy.

'Well, that does it. I'm bored to tears and pooped to high heaven to go with it,' Inspector Marklow announced. 'Folks, you've all been very factually helpful, though not in the slightest bit interesting, sorry to say. Lott, when are the boys from the mortuary arriving? Mind staying till they get here? I need to get a wriggle on. Nessa'll be on the warpath, the bleedin' warpath.'

'That . . . that's it?' Cecil Milford asked, tugging at a lock of his golden hair.

Marklow was buttoning up his overcoat, nodding and wittering about needing to get to the shops before they closed – Nessa needed another bottle of sherry for this evening – and Daphne could hold her tongue no longer.

'No, that's not bloody it!' she barked, her words caus-ing all to freeze. 'He didn't pop his clogs, Marklow; someone popped them for him. Someone had been *poisoning* him!'

Daphne adjusted her glasses, cleared her throat and took a sizable sip of the red wine that Alfred had served her. In years to come, despite the dozens of front-page stories under Daphne's name, during countless investi-gations solved and truths uncovered, this moment would remain one of Daphne's proudest. The moment she had truly left the wallflower behind.

A moment of silence passed. Baffled glances were thrown here and there across the room. Daphne surveyed the group before her. Irene Juniper began pulling at a thread in her black culottes, her eyes fixed on the floor. Donald Hartforth's eyebrows were raised in amusement. Alfred Burford bit his lip pensively, while Cecil Milford, beautiful Cecil Milford, was apparently unperturbed. Chester, meanwhile, looked shocked anew, as if struck by a second tragedy.

'Crikey. Release the kraken, is it?' Donald smirked, lighting another cigarette.

'Well, why the bleedin' hell didn't you say so, King?' Marklow sighed.

'Because nobody's let me get a word in edgeways,' Daphne muttered, smoothing down her blouse and trying to shake off the feeling that she resembled an obstreperous child.

She then explained precisely what she had found in Robert's dressing room (eyebrows were raised at the revelation that she had been, not to put too fine a point on it, snooping around) and how she knew the mushrooms to be poisonous. Marklow, unbuttoning his overcoat reluctantly, conceded that this did put rather a new complexion on events.

'You think that Robert was . . . murdered?' Chester slumped back into the chair he was occupying. 'Murdered? Robert?'

'That certainly seems to be a possibility, Chester,' Daphne replied. 'Robert's stomach pains earlier support the hypothesis: the symptoms of *Amanita virosa* mushroom poisoning take several days to make themselves known, but they're nasty little blighters. Victims experience some diarrhoea, a touch of vomiting, but nothing that would necessarily set the alarm bells ringing. All the while, however, the toxins are wheedling away at the liver, till it fails entirely. Gone, kaput, finito.'

She took another sip of her wine, finding herself warmed by both the alcohol and the sense of pride spreading through her body. These people were listening to her, really listening to her. She felt like a steam engine that, after years of chugging slowly along, restrained by regulations and encumbered by heavy loads, was now hurtling at high speed – controlled high speed, mind – towards an as yet unknown destination.

'Crikey.' Alfred ran a fidgeting hand through his already unkempt hair, his nervous grin exposing the gap in his teeth. 'That's a bit of a shocker.'

'Thank you for the multilingual explanation there, Miss King,' Donald said, 'but I'm in the dark as to why *you're* the one telling us all this. Are we to take it that you're a theatre writer by day, ace detective by night?'

Daphne blushed slightly. 'Well, I merely happen to possess certain ... skills and knowledge which lend themselves to ... solving problems of this nature. And as a matter of fact, if you really must know, I'm not a theatre writer, I'm an agony aunt.'

To hell with Halliday's insistence on her anonymity. Daphne felt certain that the time had come for that particular veil to be ripped to shreds.

Donald let out a hoot. 'Well blow me down with a feather if the plot isn't thickening by the second. Just who have you let wade into our ... *happy* little family, Chester?'

Chester's expression darkened. 'Whoever she is, she seems to be doing a jolly good job of honouring our fallen player – more than can be said of you two.' He gestured towards Donald and Irene. The latter, Daphne noted, had tightened the loose thread around her little finger so much it had gone white.

'And while we're on the topic of Miss King's unsurpassed talents, perhaps she might give you a tutorial, Inspector Marklow?' Chester now directed his ire at the police officer standing somewhat awkwardly in the doorway.

'That's, ah, kind, Chester, but we really needn't rag on

Inspector Marklow,' Daphne cut in quickly. She could little afford to have Marklow's nose out of joint at this early stage in her burgeoning career as investigative crime reporter. It would be a crying shame if she were to lose access to his contacts and intelligence – in the sense of information rather than cleverness.

'Ahem, well, as it happens, Miss King's been known to help us out a bit in the past. That . . . um duchess – no, contessa – that was quite some act you pulled off there, Daphne. But, yes, but . . . I must remind you that Miss King is not, in point of fact, a trained law enforcement officer of any kind.' Marklow's eyes darted around the room. 'However, in light of Miss King's . . . news, I think it advisable that you all leave the theatre so that our boys can conduct a thorough search of the premises. We'll need you to pop your addresses down in case we need to ask you any further questions.'

'Nice and straightforward, that one, Inspector,' Alfred said, evidently pleased to have made an uncontroversial contribution to proceedings. 'We're all staying at the Regency Hotel just round the corner on Golden Lion Street. Not quite the illustrious establishment it once was, by all accounts, but still, rather plum, all considered.'

This was news to Daphne, and pleasing news at that. All of the players under one roof would make her task rather easier. She pictured herself swanning from room to room in the hotel, a notebook under her arm, a barrage of probing questions upon her lips. *But who is this mysterious, purposeful woman on a quest for truth and justice?* the hotel staff would whisper among themselves. One particularly knowledgeable employee – possibly a French sommelier – would answer that it was the famed Daphne King, once a purveyor of household tips, now an emissary of Themis herself – Daphne for some reason fancied that sommeliers had an extensive knowledge of Greek goddesses.

'I say, Miss King, hallooo?' Alfred's voice snapped Daphne back into the here and now.

'Yes, Alfred. How may I help you?'

'I was just saying,' Alfred said, 'that perhaps you might escort me to meet my sister? She's been hunkered down in her dressing room – well, she's repurposed it as a writing studio, to be accurate – since the news earlier. I suspect she'd like to hear your take on what's been going on. You could tell her over a gin or two, and then we'll all retire to the Regency.'

Daphne ruminated for a moment. A gin with a hunkered-down writer was an appealing prospect. But she had business to attend to, so she declined Alfred's offer, adding that she would be delighted to meet his sister some time later.

Alfred insisted on pouring everyone a last glass of the

red wine, and they toasted Robert before going their separate ways: each to their own dressing room to gather what belongings they needed before, as instructed by Marklow, leaving the theatre.

Irene and Donald departed, whispering between them as they left. Alfred and Cecil drained their glasses and went soon after, followed by Inspector Marklow.

'Well, Miss King, it appears you may well have bitten off more than you can chew.' Chester chuckled feebly.

'I rather doubt it, Chester,' Daphne replied crisply, surprising herself somewhat with her certainty. Apparently, the steam engine would brook no obstacles. 'In fact, I'm quite keen to acquire more to chew on. I rather think it's time you told me all about these parcels you've been receiving.'

11

Chester sighed and glanced about the now empty bar. 'I've been expecting this.'

Daphne smiled. Here was a man alive to her nous, her nose for the curious and the unspoken. 'Oh really?'

'Yes. Nigel told me you'd been asking after them. The parcels, I mean.'

Daphne's ego deflated slightly. Of course. Nigel. Never trust a doorman.

'I promise you, I'll tell you everything I know about them. I don't know why, but I trust you, Miss King. It's a funny thing.' He chuckled again, this time wearily. 'My wife, Theodora, I must speak with her first. This has all been . . . Well, I feel as though I've been put through the ringer somewhat. Theodora will see me right. I fear I will be no help without her. Please, meet me in my dressing room in a little while. At say four o'clock?'

This gave Daphne pause. A person of interest, possessing information of interest, trying to put her off?

This was the time to tighten her grip, surely, to coax and cajole Chester into providing her with a satisfactory and comprehensive explanation of the parcels. Daphne looked at the old man, his eyes watery, his heretofore lustrous beard bedraggled after the death of his friend.

'Very well. Yes, okay,' Daphne replied. 'I'll meet you in your dressing room. But I must warn you, Chester: if you do a runner, I'll be terribly disappointed.'

He gave her a gentle smile in return. 'I rather suspect, Miss King, that the time for "doing a runner" has been and gone. Some time ago, I fear.'

Alfred had dawdled behind as the others dispersed, and, seeing Daphne's current options appeared to be either to sit alone in the bar awaiting the four o'clock assignation or accept Alfred's earlier invitation to meet his sister, she decided to take him up on his offer. Chester seemed to trust her, but her presence had provoked reactions ranging from mild curiosity to indifference to borderline hostility among the others. The more she was seen as an outsider, the less she would be told; and the less she was told, the further she was from unravelling what could, she surmised, be rather a knotty scenario.

No, alone in the bar would not do; she had acquaintances to make, information to glean. Alfred, practically skipping at being joined by Daphne, immediately commenced a rambling monologue, veering from the relative merits of each of the Pre-Raphaelites (his art professor had favoured Millais, but Alfred thought him a dour prig, favouring Rossetti), all the way back to his Christmas plans (he and his sister always spent it with each other, their parents having passed away). He concluded by asking Daphne whether she really did think that Robert had been 'done in'.

Daphne found Alfred's harmless (though frankly uninteresting) burblings a perfect accompaniment to some contemplations of her own. The day – or rather, the hours since her arrival at the Theatre Royale – had created within her from the off a sense of unease. She now found herself seized by a queer and unshakeable sense that she might have missed something. She must, at the earliest possible opportunity, jot down her swirling thoughts in her notebook. Her previous efforts in the realm of investigating had taught her that when committed to paper with pen and ink, a notion or an observation either became meaningful or was rendered inconsequential.

'Well, here we are, Miss King.' Alfred had halted outside a dressing room.

'That's so awfully schoolmarmish, Alfred. "Miss King" makes me sound like some particularly unpleasant Latin conjugations are imminent. Do call me Daphne,' she said in a breezily confident manner.

'Well, then, *Daphne*, here we are. Brace yourself.' With that, Alfred steered her into the dressing room to the left, and Daphne was enveloped by a miasma of cigarette smoke and a distinct whiff of gin. Had she allowed Alfred to usher her into some den of vice? She'd heard about opium dens all right, and they *were* on Soho's doorstep after all. A record player could be heard scratchily playing a rather modern rendition of 'Silent Night' (Daphne was certain that there hadn't been a freewheeling saxophone interlude in the original). Her glasses instantly steaming up, Daphne removed them and glanced about her. A solitary figure sat draped across an armchair in the corner of the room, a notebook in one hand, cigarette in the other. A cut-glass tumbler of gin was resting upon the end of a dressing table, lipstick smudges around the rim betraying its recent use.

'Daphne, meet my sister – the soon-to-be-trailblazing playwright Veronica Burford. Sister dearest, meet Daphne King from the *Daily Chronicle*,' Alfred declared in tones that would not have been incongruous in a butler announcing the arrival of landed gentry at a country pile.

Veronica Burford, however, was a figure whose arrival at a Sussex estate would have created a significant commotion. Where a hostess of even moderate gentility might have expected a modest skirt, Veronica sported a pair of corduroy slacks; in lieu of a tidy blouse was a billowing collarless shirt of indistinct shape. Hooded eyelids peering out from a pageboy hairstyle which framed her angular face, Veronica Burford summoned up the spirit of Greta Garbo and exuded a sullen insouciance which, as Daphne would learn, was as infuriating as it was intoxicating.

'I must warn you,' Alfred continued. 'Don't listen to a word she says. To pay heed to my sister is to dance with the devil.'

'Oh now, Alfred, how perfectly unfair of you,' came a drawling voice from the corner. 'I am *far* more interesting than Lucifer, that overrated charlatan pedalling thin contrivances and cheap chicanery.'

Veronica rose from the armchair, gathering her gin tumbler and placing her notebook in the spot previously occupied by the glass. Turning her coolly inscrutable gaze to Daphne, she approached at a deliberately unhurried pace, giving Daphne leisure to observe both the room and its inhabitant. Although the company had, she knew, only taken up residence in the Theatre Royale five days ago, the room was already littered with *objets* that betrayed Veronica's character: a cluster of leatherbound books, an empty wine bottle sporting a single sprig of holly, a crumpled playbill of what appeared to be Parisian provenance affixed to the wall beside the armchair, and an outlandishly large bunch of mistletoe in front of the mirror.

'I was under the impression that it was dear old Fabian that's had Chester and Theodora getting into a tizz the last couple of days?' Veronica asked. 'Had them both running around like headless chickens – must get things in order for Monsieur le Prince. It had tempted me to abscond, but now I'm rather glad I didn't. A gin, Miss King? A toast to the dearly departed Robert Stirling is in order, after all.'

'Veronica, you must hear what Daphne's uncovered. It's quite the thing, you know – it'll require at *least* one gin. Daphne, do fill her in, and spare none of the gory details,' Alfred entreated her.

'Uncovered? What's to uncover? I was given to understand that Robert keeled over onstage.' Veronica frowned as she sloshed liberal doses of gin into the three tumblers. 'And hang about. I thought you were here to write a lovely little piece massaging the egos of Chester and Theodora? *Uncovering* things sounds deliciously pioneering of you. Tell me, are you a cultural correspondent moonlighting as a hard-bitten investigator?'

'This was to be my first foray into cultural corresponding,' Daphne nonchalantly replied, angling herself on a stool and placing her satchel on the floor beside her. 'My bread and butter comes from attending to all manner of domestic woes. You may have seen my name wrapped around your fish and chips – Dear Susan?'

The siblings were agog. Of course they had heard of Dear Susan; she was the saviour of fretful women up and down the country. Not infrequently Veronica amused herself by reciting the musings of Dear Susan to her fellow playwrights. Veronica had pictured a woman of a certain age, bedecked in pearls, a poodle resting at her slippered feet, a husband (her third, Veronica had always fancied; the first two killed in tragically heroic accidents) mowing the lawn outside. Yet here she was before them, chipped gin tumbler in hand, unruly hair, bitten nails and a broken umbrella.

'I thought my capacity for surprise had been exhausted by three years living in Berlin,' Veronica said, folding her left leg over the right, shaking her head in wonderment. 'Yet I find myself outdone. How very refreshing, Miss King. Now, you must *swear* to tell us everything about the Gambling Contessa; leave no detail by the wayside. We must hear how, when, where and why on earth you realised she'd been spirited away to Monte Carlo and was in dire need of Dear Susan's assistance.'

Daphne smiled. Perhaps Dear Susan wasn't quite such a millstone after all. 'Well, it was all quite easy really, once I had . . .'

She stopped herself. *Concentrate, Daphne.* Allowing herself to be flattered by a bohemian playwright was *not* the order of the day. 'Actually, I think it would be a rather better use of our time to discuss Robert Stirling's death.'

With that, Daphne provided Veronica with a succinct – yet still colourful – precis of her discovery of the mushrooms.

'Well, bust my buttons. You truly believe it was a slaying? A murder? That Robert Stirling was killed?' Veronica gave no further appearance of nonchalance, but leaned forward, cradling her gin in her hands as she gazed at Daphne unblinkingly.

'I do believe that, yes.'

Veronica exhaled. 'Well, plenty out there would like to see Robert in a spot of bother, I shouldn't wonder.'

'Come again?' Daphne recalled Irene Juniper's allusions. 'You'll have to spell that out for me, I'm afraid.'

Alfred handed them both another round of gins, then adjusted the gramophone.

'No, sorry, Alfred, I must draw the line at "Good King Wenceslas". Find something else, please,' Veronica implored, before turning back to Daphne and raising an eyebrow. 'Well, there's no love lost between Robert and, well, rather a lot of women out there. Something of a roué, by all accounts.'

Daphne frowned. 'A womaniser, you mean?'

'Why yes, as a matter of fact, I do mean that. Always a fan of a woman who calls a spade a spade,' Veronica said, swirling the gin in her glass. 'Yes, it's well known that dear departed Robert left quite a legion of spurned, wronged and generally rather ill-treated women in his wake.'

Daphne remembered once again Irene's threat: *I am not staying here if he is!*

'Tell me, is Irene Juniper one of those ill-treated women?' she asked, maintaining a level gaze.

'Irene?! Lord! Shouldn't think so!' Alfred blurted. 'Robert's been a swine in the past, but he's in his dotage now – well, was in his dotage.'

Daphne kept her eyes fixed on Veronica.

'It's not my place to . . . You should speak to Irene,' Veronica said, her voice uncertain for the first time since Daphne had met her.

'I absolutely intend to.' Could Irene Juniper really be a suspect? She had certainly given every appearance of loathing Robert Stirling. But murder him? Daphne really couldn't say. And precisely because she really couldn't say, Daphne knew that Irene couldn't be expelled from the clouds of suspicion gathering in her mind.

'If I may ask, Veronica, your role in this production is . . .?' Daphne enquired.

Veronica curled her lips with no attempt to mask her disdain. Alfred, nearly choking on a mouthful of gin, spluttered, 'Oh Lord, now you've done it.'

'I am responsible for . . . cobbling together this *adaptation* of *A Christmas Carol*,' Veronica began, slinking back to her armchair. 'Of course, it's a means to an end. Chester's an old family friend. Heard that I'd . . . run out of luck in Berlin, so asked if I'd be so kind as to do him the honour of carving up *A Christmas Carol*, chucking away most of the innards, and putting it back together for him. Couldn't say no, really. All said and done, quite enjoyed taking the shears to it, plucking out two hours' worth of bon mots and squeezing the characters down to a cast of four. No takers in London for my *true* work – yet.'

'Veronica's been in Berlin for the last few years, Daphne.' Alfred was evidently accustomed to adopting the role of interpreter for his sister's more gnomic pronouncements. 'She delights in telling everyone that all she's been doing is carousing with poets and frequenting nightclubs and bordellos.'

'A girl has to have her fun,' Veronica chipped in, an arch smile spreading across her face. She then went on to outline the concept of her play: a nine-hour cycle uniting the women of Greek tragedy – Electra, Antigone, Medea and Andromache – in the afterlife. A nine-hour howl of catharsis and anguish that aimed to both highlight the artifice of theatre and the unreality of reality.

'Not exactly one for the Saturday matinee audience, I

wouldn't say,' Veronica concluded, taking a satisfied final swig of her gin. 'I've asked Chester to cast his eye over it, see if he can't make it a touch more . . . marketable. He managed it with *A Woman of Grace and Fury*, and, though I shan't be making any unnecessary sacrifices, I'm not above a compromise if it means I'll get my *true* work on the stage here. Anyway, I'll keep chasing the old bugger. Not been terribly forthcoming with his writerly advice thus far.'

'Speaking of Chester –' Daphne glanced at her wristwatch '– I've an appointment with him, and I'm a little late. Care to escort me?'

There was something about the Burford siblings that told Daphne she could rely on their candour. She just had to hope that her assessment of them was correct.

Just as Daphne was rearranging her satchel for perhaps the seventeenth time that day, the door to the room was flung open. A compact, stocky man stood there, his body visibly tense as if braced for combat.

'Chrissakes,' he spat in an American accent. 'It's a quarter after four. What're ya waitin' for, ya packa clowns?'

12

Apparently alone in her perturbation at this interruption, Daphne leaped from the stool. Conscious of the cigarette smoke hanging in the air and the surely unmistakable fug of gin wafting from their persons, Daphne's cheeks flushed with embarrassment at enjoying herself far too much while on the job.

The man eyed the scene with a glare shark-like in its inscrutability and intensity. His bearing suggested the contained kinetic energy of a particularly unfriendly jack-in-the-box, gleefully awaiting any inept behaviour, which would trigger – or justify – an explosion. Although at least three inches shorter than anyone else present, he was remarkably imposing. Broad-shouldered in his navy-blue pinstripe suit (the pink lily in the jacket pocket of which struck an odd note of incongruity), he tsk'd loudly, his flinty face animated by disapproval.

'C'mon,' he ordered gruffly, turning his glare on

Daphne. 'Chester told you four o'clock. You're late. Chester and Theodora are waitin'.'

With that he turned briskly, emitting a sharp whistle. Veronica sighed laboriously and hoisted herself out of the armchair, while Alfred turned to Daphne with wide eyes, biting his lower lip.

'Oh dear. When Mr Salter makes an appearance, it's invariably because some unpleasantness or other has also made an appearance,' he said nervously.

Daphne was intrigued. Exactly what manner of 'unpleasantness' was Alfred anticipating?

As if in answer to her unspoken question, Veronica said reassuringly, 'Don't mind Mr Salter. He does have something of a penchant for dramatic entrances and . . . eloquent proclamations. We try not to take him too seriously – suggest you follow suit.'

'All the same, Veronica,' her brother countered, 'perhaps we ought to apprise Daphne of the situation before we . . .'

A moment passed, during which the siblings seemed to be communicating on a plane entirely removed from Daphne. Veronica, self-possessed, measured, fixed her brother with an even stare. Alfred, meanwhile, was blinking rapidly and had hooked his thumbs into his belt loops, his fingers waggling distractingly.

'Oh the situation? You must mean the situation

regarding the parcels that Chester's been receiving – the ones that appear to exert a malevolent force upon all who speak their name?' Daphne said. 'I sincerely hope you're not expecting to dangle the promise of "unpleasantness" before a journalist and expect her to sit tight with a tumbler of gin while the good stuff happens offstage. Shall we?'

Daphne's assertiveness put paid to further prevarication on the part of the siblings. With a resigned shrug, Alfred made way for his sister, who, naturally, headed the trio out of the dressing room. For the first time since meeting her, Daphne noticed a flicker of uncertainty dance across Veronica's face as she paused outside, a hint that her self-assurance was not entirely unassailable.

'Daphne, word to the wise,' Veronica said in a portentous tone. 'Theodora can be rather . . . protective of Chester. Particularly so in recent weeks. These parcels have really given them the willies. And now Robert . . . Well, you can imagine.'

Daphne nodded vaguely at Veronica, adjusting her glasses in a way which she felt suited the role of a serious investigative journalist not in the slightest squiffy after unaccustomed mid-afternoon gin.

Arriving outside another dressing room, Veronica threw a glance at her brother, who knocked tentatively at the door. A muffled response was heard, its gruff tenor indicating that it emanated from the bullish Mr Salter. Interpreting this as an invitation to enter, Veronica led the way. As she did so, its three inhabitants – Chester Harrison, a smile too glacial to be convincing upon his face, the mysterious Mr Salter, eyes narrowed, and the rather awe-inspiringly imperious Theodora D'Arby – abruptly stopped talking.

Larger than the room that Veronica had made hers, this one was heavy with the smell of flowers, bouquets perched here and there around a chaise longue that occupied one end of the space. That the chaise had seen better days could not be denied. Through its well-worn covers came whisps of stuffing, while a melange of off-putting stains and scorches on the armrest suggested that previous occupants had been both partial to red wine and careless with their cigarettes. Beside it, covered entirely by an unsightly doily, was a very small table, not quite high enough to be useful for resting one's drink. Perhaps explaining the wine stains on the chaise longue.

None of the other customary trifles and trappings of backstage glamour here, Daphne noted. No perfume bottles or gilt-framed photographs beside the dressing mirrors, only a battered tin promising it contained McFarlane & Sturgess Finest Biscuits. The costume hangers were empty but for Chester's red scarf and tweed coat, and a fox cape which, Daphne concluded, must belong to Theodora D'Arby. The room was enveloped in an atmosphere of friction – perhaps domestic, possibly professional, certainly unresolved – that was as palpable and as overpowering as the scent of lilies.

In the full-length mirror upon the wall opposite, Daphne caught a glimpse of herself and immediately rearranged her quizzical expression into something far more neutral and benign.

Chester greeted her, extending a frail hand towards her.

'Daphne, Miss King,' he said. 'Your patience today has not gone unrecognised, nor has it gone unappreciated. Thank you for allowing me an interlude to speak with my wife. I hope you'll now find me more . . . willing and able to furnish you with all you need. Robert's death has left me . . . bereft. Overcome. I hope you'll continue to be patient with me in this most trying of times.'

Daphne nodded her assent.

Theodora D'Arby cut a formidable figure. Steely-eyed, fists clenched, she had halted in the middle of the room when Daphne, Veronica and Alfred entered – evidently, she had been pacing back and forth. Her sombre green dress trailed on the somewhat grubby carpet, her shoes discarded beneath the chaise longue. London's Theatreland had been abuzz with rumours of

Theodora's descent into decrepitude since her return from Hollywood, and Daphne was, of course, familiar with this clothesline prattle and had seasoned it with a tablespoon of salt. Now Daphne was furnished with definitive evidence that the rumour mill should be demolished and on its site a shrine built. For Theodora D'Arby, supposedly over the hill at the age of forty-four, radiated a magisterial form of beauty that called to mind an oracle, a siren . . . Daphne found herself unable to tear her eyes away from the woman whose performance as Joan of Arc, that timeless incarnation of ethereality and might, had proved so captivating at the outset of her career.

'Good afternoon, Miss D'Arby. I'm Daphne King,' she stated plainly. 'Here from the *Chronicle*. I was there when Robert died. It was I who found the poisoned mushrooms in his dressing room and told the police about them. I know there's something going on here – perhaps a number of things – and, as a start, I would like to know more about these parcels.'

Theodora's chill appeared to thaw a little, impressed by Daphne's refusal to quake before her *froideur*. She presented Daphne with a cool smile, neither too enthusiastic nor too lacklustre, the kind of smile that had for years been lazily (but not inaccurately) described as sphinx-like by those reporters fortunate enough to have been granted an audience with her.

'You must excuse us, Miss King,' she purred. 'You find us in the midst of . . . a trying episode.' 'Trying' was, it appeared, Theodora's diplomatic synonym for gloomy, dispiriting, tense, potentially murderous.

'Dora, let's hold off spilling the beans to the press, no?' Mr Salter said, a wheedling undertone slipping into his hitherto truculent tones.

At this Daphne was finally, formally introduced to the curious Mr Salter – or, to adopt Theodora's description, 'darling, dour George'.

'Can't think how I should have survived at all in Hollywood without darling, dour George's firm hand on the tiller. To overstretch the metaphor, devilish treacherous waters, Miss King,' Theodora explained, as she glided with remarkable elegance across the unsightly carpet towards the chaise. 'A person could drown in all the hogwash and hysteria. Mercifully, George came to my rescue – threw me a lifebelt, so to speak. I did warn you that I would overstretch the metaphor.'

A playful wink from Theodora indicated that she had momentarily forgotten the 'trying episode' in which she was enmired. She arranged herself on the chaise longue.

'You mustn't mind him, Miss King. Gets into terrible huffs now and then. A Hollywood agent marooned with an enfeebled stage actress in rainy London at Christmas,' Theodora continued, a delicate sigh escaping her mouth. 'And I shouldn't wonder that darling, dour George thinks London as dull as ditch water compared to Hollywood.'

George allowed himself a brief smile, shooting the cuffs of his shirt beyond the sleeves of his pinstriped suit. 'Ain't nothing dull about this country of yours. Never-ending puzzles. Bangers and mash, apples and pears, cop a flower pot. You limeys and yer riddles.'

Chester and Theodora both smiled warmly at Mr Salter's apparently affectionate tribute. Smiled as though they had rid themselves of the memory of Robert Stirling's dead body, just an hour or so ago, lying cold on the stage beyond their dressing room. Once more that day, and not for the final time, the mercurial nature of actors came to the front of Daphne's mind. A mystifying lot, though, she conceded, not without their charms.

'Do excuse my frankness, Chester, but would you mind telling me what's been going on?' Daphne returned them to the task at hand.

Theodora glanced at her husband, prompting Chester to pat her hand reassuringly. 'Dora's a little wary about you, Miss King. Hope you'll forgive her caution.'

'Of course,' Daphne replied. 'I'm a journalist, and I know we've a certain reputation: tawdry sensation mongers and callous headline hunters. I can assure you, Miss D'Arby, that I seek one thing and one thing only: the truth. I shan't gloss over anything unpalatable, but I certainly shan't luxuriate in it. Nor will I permit any untruths to be printed in the *Chronicle*.'

There was that steam-engine energy again. Daphne would have been wrongfooted by her own eloquence and certainty if she hadn't been concentrating very much on not being wrongfooted by the gin.

'You can tell me everything, or you can tell me nothing – or something in between,' Daphne continued. 'I've a feeling – and I suspect that you share it – that whatever has happened, or is happening, will reach the newspapers somehow. The question is whether you would like me to convey it to the public first, or else wait for someone less discriminating and trustworthy to root it out.'

That glowing sensation was growing within her. She felt that yes, she could discover the truth. More than that – she *would* discover the truth. It was colossal cheek barging in here, staking her claim to whatever it was they were hiding. But Daphne had never felt so sure of anything in her life.

'My dear, you've missed your calling; you really ought to be a saleswoman. I can just picture you behind a counter at Selfridges, convincing hordes of poor, unsuspecting housewives to hand over their cash in exchange for some snake oil,' Theodora drawled. 'We still can't be entirely sure what *did* happen to Robert, but my husband appears to have a fondness for you, and it's evident that Veronica and Alfred seem to have taken a shine to you as well. On the basis of which I find myself struck by an inclination to trust you. You've a gutsiness that appeals to one and I rather think an intelligence that might do some good around here.'

Chester spluttered slightly, placing his cup on the side next to one of the more lurid bouquets. Dabbing his mouth with a handkerchief, he began, 'I'm having second thoughts about this. Perhaps it's really nothing we need to worry ourselves about – certainly nothing we need trouble Daphne with.'

Theodora elevated herself from her reclining position – for really, 'elevate' is the only verb applicable to a movement so agile – and moved to place an affectionate hand on her husband's arm.

'Darling, believe me when I say that I would far rather put this entire business behind us, but the fact of the matter is that we probably do have every reason to concern ourselves with the contents of these . . . parcels you have been receiving since September. The parcels that arrived once a week at first, now . . . daily.' Theodora appeared weary and she closed her eyes momentarily.

'I wish to high heaven I knew who the blackguard was.' Alfred's endearingly archaic insult was at odds with the strength of the hostility he evidently felt towards the perpetrator of the offences. 'Perfectly indecent to be hounding you like this, Chester, and you, Theodora.'

'Vulgar and, may I say, unoriginal pranks,' Chester dismissed. 'Nothing more than that. Some nasty bugger having a laugh at our expense.'

Daphne, tired of trying to piece together the pieces of the puzzle that had been scattered thus far, decided this was the moment to bring the shilly-shallying to an end. 'So they contained . . . *what*, exactly?'

'Oh bravo, Miss King. Right to the point.' Theodora laughed not unkindly. 'I shan't debase myself to go into detail, but these are not offerings of admiration and gratitude. Offerings of *that* nature I have seen before. When I was performing in Paris, or on Broadway. *These*, on the other hand –' she gestured to some unseen and unappealing pile of gifts '– are most unsavoury.'

'Wine and cigars, for the most part,' Chester said. 'Expensive ones too. Nice. Tasteful. But packaged up with rather less nice accompaniments. A scattering of dead cockroaches. A shrivelled up slug. In one, a decomposing rat.'

'How queer,' Daphne said thoughtfully. 'Cockroaches, slugs, rats – pests all of them. And expensive wine and cigars? A prankster not shy about spending money on the finer things. What sort of wine? And don't suppose anyone can recall the cigar brand? That could be a jolly useful nugget of information, you see – I have a friend – well, I say friend, acquaintance, really – in Green Park who knows all the chaps in the cigar business . . .'

A flood of questions poured forth from Daphne. Were the parcels postmarked or hand-delivered? At what time of day had they arrived? Presumably the stage door manager could shed light on the mode of delivery, perhaps even furnish them with a description of who had delivered them. The parcels seemed peculiarly personal; could Chester think of anyone who might have a motive to do such a thing? Someone with a score to settle, someone who wanted to remind Chester of something? Garden slugs, or more exotic? German cockroaches or brown-banded cockroaches? A black rat or was it brown?

'Specificity really is the key,' Daphne explained. 'Helps one to unlock all manner of riddles.'

The stale taste of gin was still in her mouth. She really would have to get some water after this.

'Do you know, Daphne, you raise some highly significant points,' Chester enthused as warmly as he could. 'But, unfortunately, so repelled were we by the *gifts* that we disposed of them as swiftly as possible. I think the cigars were Imperial, though chucked 'em immediately. Can't stand the things any more.'

Daphne noted the 'any more'. 'And when was it that you *could* stand the things?'

Chester bristled slightly. 'Many years ago – many, *many* years ago. As to . . . enemies,' he continued, 'I fear that envy is a hazard of my profession. It could be any number of . . . rivals who feel that they have been passed over. Or perhaps a fan, an over-ardent fan seeking to establish a connection with me, however unsettling a connection.'

Chester was flailing, filling the room with suggestions and hints that he seemed to hope were plausible, but Daphne sensed there was also something he was withholding.

'And today's parcel, have you opened it yet?' she asked.

13

Shaking his head, Chester reached behind the chaise longue to retrieve a cardboard box.

'May I?' Daphne said, reaching out for the box. Chester handed it over.

Opening it with a delicacy that one might reserve for handling a newborn lamb or a Fabergé egg, Daphne laid aside a dead cockroach (brown-banded, she noted) and removed the latest offering: neither wine nor cigars, it was, in fact, a fountain pen.

Daphne examined it closely. Expensive. In almost pristine condition. It had been used, yes, but sparingly; the nib gave no indication of having had pressure applied to it for any prolonged period of time.

While the inhabitants of the room watched her, Daphne's mind wove together the scant facts with which she'd been furnished, each one bringing with it several pressing questions. She glanced up at Chester. His face had drained of colour.

'The pen – you've seen it before, Chester? It means something to you?'

Chester shook his head vigorously, but no words emerged from his lips.

He was lying, Daphne was sure of it. The pen had significance; she'd eat her hat if it didn't. His face possessed the haunted look of Scrooge confronted by the Ghost of Christmas Past. This pen was a spectral visitation, a reminder. A prompt. A threat.

Daphne turned her attention to the box that the pen had arrived in. It was entirely nondescript: no markings, no stamp. Theodora explained that it had been found outside, as with previous boxes, beside the stage door by Nigel. The only detail that marked it out as an item not destined for the rubbish was the neat, handwritten label affixed to it: '*FAO Mr Chester Harrison, writer*'.

Quizzically, Daphne glanced up at Chester and Theodora. 'And no note, no letter? No . . . nothing? And hang about – why only "Chester Harrison, *writer*"? Why not "Chester Harrison, *writer and director*"? I was under the impression that you . . . well, that you were more successful as a director?'

A shrug of the shoulders from Chester – bereft of his usual loquacity – indicated that no, there had been no note.

'How very queer,' Daphne murmured to herself. She was overcome by an intuition that facts were being concealed from her.

Chester and Theodora locked eyes for a moment, and Daphne found herself looking away, her investigative instincts overtaken by a sense of decorum.

Veronica exhaled, as if she had been reluctant to breathe during the discovery of the pen. 'Look. Chester's probably right. It's some fruitcake admirer of his desperate for attention. Probably one of the twinset brigade, a prim old dowager named Maud who's losing her marbles and wants to lavish some presents on the lip-smackingly handsome Chester Harrison before she kicks the bucket. Pen's probably a family heirloom that her son – no doubt a banker – will search high and low for, then sack the maid, believing her to have sold it to fund her wedding to a ne'er-do-well who'll break her heart and steal all the silverware.'

Daphne heard a giggle and, to her astonishment, realised that it had emerged from her.

'When you frame it in such melodramatic terms, I for one am on tenterhooks to see what Maud the marble-losing dowager is going to produce next,' Daphne said lightly, forcing a smile.

Theodora and Chester were evidently less satisfied

with Veronica's speculations. The wine, the cigars – mention of these previous offerings had dented Chester's bluster very little. This pen, however, appeared to have thrown an entirely new shade over proceedings. A darker shade. It seemed to Daphne that the pen signalled the arrival of a critical point in events.

Chester stood up uncertainly, placing his cup back on the side.

'Time, dear friends, is not on our side, regrettably. Inspector Marklow told us to be out by half past four, and we have outstayed our welcome. This –' he approached Daphne and carefully took the pen from her '– I shall keep in here, safely under lock and key. Just in case dowager Maud comes knocking.'

Planting a kiss on his wife's cheek, Chester suggested that they all retire to the bar at the Regency Hotel. He was, he admitted, out of sorts, but he felt that some drinks were in order. To steady the nerves, toast Robert. Theodora wore a mask of resignation. George grunted and glugged down the remaining Scotch in his glass.

Daphne nodded her agreement, though she had a feeling in the pit of her (still empty) stomach that there was something she was missing. And her limited experience had taught her at least one lesson so far: when one is raw and out of sorts, one is honest and unguarded. No matter. She would have her chance to poke a little more at this pen business and everything that had clearly preceded it.

Alfred, meanwhile, turned to his sister and Daphne. 'Don't know about you, but I think we're all ready for a lie-down after that, wouldn't you say?'

14

Walking had always served as stimulant and sedative for Daphne, as the circumstances required. In the evenings, should frustrations or regrets, hypotheses or suppositions rattle through her mind, it was in the hushed streets of Camberwell that she sought solace. Rarely an ambler, never an idler, Daphne's walks were brisk in pace, giving the impression of purpose even on those numerous occasions when she set off with no particular route in mind, much less a destination. When entwined in the tendrils of any thorny predicament (the strange case of the missing greyhound three years ago sprang to mind), a bracing march to Nunhead could be relied upon to liberate her.

And so it was that, rather than head immediately to the Regency Hotel, Daphne had instead retrieved her coat and satchel, and made her way out into the streets of Soho.

Darkness had fallen and the snow had, for the time

being at least, retreated. Turning right out of the theatre, she approached Shaftesbury Avenue. With three days until Christmas Day, the streets were dotted with scuttling pedestrians, some laden with shopping bags, others desperately empty-handed. If Daphne headed right, she would be swept along with the crowds drawn towards the blazing lights of Piccadilly Circus. No, she decided, better to turn left, away from the thrum of the shopping hordes, towards Cambridge Circus.

As she strode past theatres and kiosks, Daphne endeavoured to arrange today's happenings in her mind. The few hours since her meeting with Martin Halliday had passed in something of a blur. There were the knowns: that Robert had died, most likely killed by mushroom poisoning. That Chester was receiving mysterious parcels. That Chester was hiding something about these parcels. That Robert had, perhaps, several enemies who would rejoice to see him harmed. Then there were the unknowns. Manifold and puzzling unknowns. Who was sending the parcels? Who had poisoned Robert? Were they one and the same person? If so, who? And why? If not, who? And why? *Oh blast it*, Daphne thought. She was running herself around in circles.

In fact, were Martin Halliday to ask Daphne what conclusions she had come to thus far, she would struggle to cobble together even the most feeble of offerings. Her encounters with Donald Hartforth and Irene Juniper had been superficial and fleeting, two vain actors primping and preening, while Cecil Milford had been dashing but silent; perspicacious though she was, not even Daphne had been able to piece together a cogent portrait of him. That would have to come later, Daphne decided. The Burford siblings, a paint-stained and energetic art-student-cum-assistant-stage-manager and an intimidatingly self-assured experimental playwright in lipstick and corduroys – well, they were of interest on a personal level, but Daphne had no idea if they were involved.

She would need to spend more time with the entire company. She was certain that some among them knew more than they were saying. Turning off Shaftesbury Avenue and into Frith Street, Daphne revisited the peculiar interlude in Chester and Theodora's dressing room. That feeling was rising again. The butterflies of doubt fluttered in her stomach. Chester's strangely muted response, Theodora's evident anxiety. George Salter's protective attitude towards his client.

Hunger assailed her once more, prompting Daphne to hesitate in her stride, but to stop for a sandwich seemed frivolous while there were still innumerable questions to be asked. As she deliberated, some plump flakes of snow began to swirl once more beneath the yellow glow of the street lamp. Daphne had her answer: she must seek refuge and she must seek sustenance. A Lyons tea shop was just ahead, red tinsel framing windows which were invitingly steamed by the warmth within. A cup of tea, a sandwich, that would see her right. Then she would head to the hotel, ready to charm, to inveigle and excavate, and to find out what the blazes that pen signified.

Slightly stale bread notwithstanding, the pit stop served its purpose adequately, and Daphne had to concede that the mince pie was of unassailable quality. Half an hour later, snowflakes swirling, Daphne decided to take one further detour on her route to the hotel. She looped back on herself and stood on the corner opposite the Theatre Royale, where a scrum of reporters were jostling for the best position.

Word had emerged that tonight's London premiere of *A Christmas Carol* was to be cancelled. Up and down Theatreland, critics who had previously been rejoicing in speculation about whether the show would be a hit or a flop were now rejoicing at another more tantalising reality: Robert Stirling's untimely death onstage, mid-rehearsal. Too delicious to be true, yet true it was. While the critics tapped out obituaries for the deceased, the press mob proper had descended upon the theatre, baying for blood – or at least an exclusive comment from one of the cast. Just along the pavement Donald

Hartforth's fans clustered around the stage door, yearning to meet the man himself. All were peered down upon by a poster depicting Robert Stirling at his most cantankerous and Scrooge-like.

The stage of the Theatre Royale had borne witness to historic events. It was here that Sir William Gosforth's Lear had brought audiences to raptures of pity and sorrow during his legendary run of 297 consecutive performances in 1903. During the Great War the building had been requisitioned for use as temporary munitions storage – and was supposed to have held shells that were used at the Somme. After the victory on the Western Front, an infamous revue was staged, which united all classes in their appreciation of long-legged dancers.

Surveying the mob, Daphne could just make out Jamie Jenkins, her weaselly nemesis, hunched in his coat, snout to the air in search of a scandal that he could scribble about for the *Chronicle*. Daphne wondered if he knew that she, Dear Susan, overlooked agony aunt for that same newspaper, was in fact conducting her own investigations into the events. And that she, Daphne King, was the one who was going to get to the root of it all.

15

Inside the Regency Hotel, Theodora glanced up from the glass of mulled wine she'd been cradling for some time now, and pursed her lips, which still bore the deep crimson colour she had painted on them earlier that day. A rather half-hearted rendition of 'God Rest Ye Merry Gentlemen' was being tapped out by the bored-looking pianist in the corner of the bar. The place really had entered a sorry state of decline since Theodora's last stay here; she found herself feeling depressed by its threadbare appearance. The clientele, once glamorous and glittering, now looked as frayed and worn as the furniture. When in London, Theodora and Chester had always favoured the Regency owing to its location in an unusually quiet pocket of the West End, a square previously untroubled by the crowds of the busier streets and favoured instead by London's intelligentsia. Theodora might once have stopped for a cocktail in the hotel lounge with a playwright, or joined a producer there for afternoon tea; now, however, the room was filled with the pianist's apparently limited repertoire of carols and the desultory chatter of middle-aged couples who had very little to say to one another.

Chester was clinking his signet ring against his glass, and the actors around Theodora sat listlessly. Chester let out a sound somewhere between a harrumph and a snort.

'Do drink your wine, Chester. If Robert knew you'd been nursing that thimble for thirty-five minutes, he really would vow to haunt you for the rest of your days,' Theodora said playfully.

Chester smiled at Theodora as she stilled his hand, rescuing his glass from the sustained attack of his signet ring. Luminous as ever, calming as ever, she gazed at him with the piercing eyes that had held him captive since he had first seen her onstage as a ferocious Joan of Arc. Two truths had struck him at that moment, some twenty years ago: she would be his star, and she would be his wife. Chester prodded at the copy of the *Standard* on the table next to him; he had, in a fit of masochism, flicked to the page containing Tyrone Bridge's piece from that morning.

'Why the *Standard* still prints that little toad's twaddle is a mystery to me.' Theodora continued, 'Society tittle-tattle and theatrical witticisms are one thing, gossip-mongering nastiness is quite another. Ignore it, Chester. We ignored him before, and we'll ignore him again. Although nothing would bring me more joy than giving him a piece of my mind the next time we have the misfortune of being in the same room as him.'

She summoned a waiter over, and, pinching the newspaper between forefinger and thumb, drawled, 'Be a dear and dispose of this somewhere – preferably in a gutter. Best place for it.'

The waiter, whose limp Father Christmas hat only underscored the decidedly unmerry atmosphere of the lounge, took the newspaper and retreated.

'Of course, we'll have to give Robert a sublime send-off.' Chester's voice had regained some of its power, the thought of celebrating his friend's career enlivening him. 'Gather all the old gang, what's left of us . . .'

Daphne bounded up to the group, observing the malaise which pervaded the scene. Alfred and Cecil were deep in conversation, Veronica appeared to be bored witless, while Irene and Donald were, as usual, engaged in conspiratorial whispering.

'Hello all,' Daphne greeted them, to an indistinct chorus of replies.

'Pull up a pew, Miss King, pull up a pew,' Chester said. 'I was just . . . I was just telling Dora that I ought to give Robert a good send-off. Least I can do after—'

'Darling, stop.' Was that a note of agitation in Theodora's voice? A suggestion of impatience?

Daphne squinted at her, as though this might enable her to understand the nuances of her tone.

'There's nothing you could have done. He's castigating himself for . . . not realising that Robert might have got himself into a spot of bother with someone. Doesn't surprise me a jot, though. Robert had a way of . . . rubbing people up the wrong way.' Theodora had inclined her head towards Daphne slightly as she explained. Daphne's face must have betrayed her faint surprise at this accusation, this allusion to misdeeds, for Theodora hurriedly added, 'Not, of course, to speak ill of the dead.'

A bizarre honking noise echoed across the bar. The sound had been produced by Irene Juniper, who was . . . laughing. A most curious turn of events. When she spoke, Irene spat out her words with unconcealed arrogance. 'Speak ill of the dead?' she began, conscious of the sensation she was causing. 'Gosh no, we'd best not do that eh, Theodora? Best not upset the apple cart, kick a hornets' nest. No, keep everything hush-hush.'

Theodora sat perfectly still. Not a muscle in her face moved; her piercing eyes were fixed on Irene. Were Daphne so inclined, she might have called it a basilisk stare, but to attach to her nominal hostess and interview subject such a loaded description would, she reflected, be unfair. And so it remained a blank stare. Irene, on the other hand, had contorted her face into a terrible pastiche of a grin.

'Darling –' Theodora's voice was perfectly contained, but she could not quite quell the icy tone that threatened to overwhelm it '– when you've jumped through as many hoops as I have, kowtowed to as many pompous drunks – or worse – who have industry clout, and generally bitten one's tongue in the face of idiocy and ridicule – well, then, my darling, you'll quite understand that one is entitled to make passing remarks about, and indeed feel . . . *niggled* by, the foibles of one's oldest friends.'

Theodora clearly judged that the conversation was closed and thus returned to murmuring soothing sounds to her husband. Irene's eye-roll indicated that she was less content with the conclusion of the interaction. She whispered something to Donald, before rushing out of the bar.

Hello, thought Daphne, before leaping up and following her.

Stepping into the square outside, Daphne realised quite how oppressively claustrophobic the bar had been. The moonlight was streaming down, and although the snow had stopped falling the chill in the air had grown.

Daphne pulled her coat tighter about her, and trotted through the snow as swiftly as she could to catch up with Irene.

'Wait, Irene, wait!' she called. Daphne had always considered herself a walker of impressive speed and stamina. She was not, however, a member of the Ladies' League of Health and Beauty, and therefore found herself panting where Irene was showing no discernible signs of exertion.

'Miss King, I'd like to be alone,' Irene said primly, refusing to slow down.

'Please, Irene,' Daphne began, 'I think you can help me. I think there's something queer going on.'

Irene halted.

Relief flooded Daphne, who suspected she could not have maintained the pace for much longer. The garden of the square lay to their right. 'Can we sit down? Talk?'

Irene sighed before allowing herself to be led into the garden by Daphne. In the summer it was an oasis of greenery straddling Soho and Shaftesbury Avenue, and now the flower beds were home to an inviting blanket of fresh snow.

Brushing snow from the nearest bench, the pair sat down, Daphne huddled against the chill, Irene's posture in line with her League training.

'They're a pack of liars, all of them,' Irene said, her

voice contemptuous. 'Lies and more lies. Robert, Theodora, Chester – all of them.'

Daphne listened intently. Irene was speaking calmly now, none of the histrionics that had animated her earlier.

'People are hiding things. People think I'm a fool, a bimbo. But I'm not, Daphne. I see things. I hear things.' Irene's anger was palpable.

'Go on. What things? Irene, if there's anything you've seen or heard, it could be helpful, it could lead to whoever killed Robert.'

Irene snorted. 'I don't care about that. He deserved what he got. Had it coming. A lecherous old man – always trying it on with me, always chancing it. Not just me, either. Vile old sod.'

Daphne nodded. 'If it's not about finding out who killed Robert, what *do* you want?'

'I want people to know what they're like – what they're really like. I've never trusted Chester and Theodora. Well, okay, I trusted them at first. I trust Lilian – my agent – and she told me it was a job worth taking, valuable experience with two veterans. But things have been happening.' Irene frowned. 'Chester flying off the handle or getting into strange funks. I know, I know, he's a director – they're not what I'd call the most stable creatures around. But these were . . . different. Always the first day when we arrived at a new theatre. He'd disappear for hours before we'd see him again.'

Daphne quickly reached into her satchel and brought out her notebook. 'Do you mind if I . . .?' Daphne gestured with her pen. 'Tell me – what's the tour been like? It's been barely five minutes since I met everyone. I feel rather at sea to be honest. But you – well, it's been what, three months on tour?'

Irene nodded before continuing. Her hands were resting on her knees, her body entirely still. 'Donald and I stuck together; we've known each other through Lilian for years. The atmosphere was . . . off. Cecil didn't seem to notice it, but then Cecil doesn't notice much. Away with the fairies, that boy. Anyway. Robert, Chester, Theodora – they stuck together too. Didn't talk to us much. Veronica and Alfred, they're good eggs; she's a bit trying, but still, good eggs generally.'

Daphne felt her judgement vindicated by the confirmation that Veronica was a good egg.

'It's been rather bloody frustrating, if I'm honest,' Irene said. 'Yes, Donald and I had each other, and Lilian would visit to watch us in every new town, take us out for a slap-up dinner. Or as slap-up as you can find in some of those backwaters. But I'm a twenty-five-year-old woman, the prime of my life. When I'm old and grey in ten years do I really want to look back and remember these years as ones I spent hobbling around in a third-rate production pretending to be a Victorian urchin boy?'

Daphne resisted the impulse to protest that at thirty-five one really wasn't old and grey (she herself had thus far been afflicted by precisely zero grey hairs), and to correct the reference to a Victorian urchin boy: Tiny Tim was no urchin. Tact dictated that she steer clear of contradicting Irene – she needed to keep her sweet. Instead, she cultivated the impression of a priest, nodding sagely as a lost soul unburdened herself of her woes.

'Mmm, yes, I can imagine.' Daphne produced a rough approximation of what she thought would equate to noises of reassurance and encouragement. 'Any particular incidents from the tour that stand out? Anything peculiar?'

'Nothing peculiar, nothing that I haven't seen before. Spats here and there, but that's to be expected. Frustrations, of course. All of us were frustrated. Chester wanted to be the Big I Am, but, and I'll be honest, Daphne, he just isn't what he used to be. Well, what everyone tells me he used to be. He's just not that ... good at his job, to be frank. And Donald couldn't stand that Robert had the title role. Theodora ... well, she looked bored to tears most of the time.'

Ambition and envy and rivalry. Threads to be pulled.

'Then of course we came to London. Things changed here. Yesterday afternoon Chester wanted to rehearse some scenes with the four of us – me, Donald, Cecil, Robert – and all went off without a hitch. Chester seemed a little distracted, but otherwise he was in finer spirits than usual. Afterwards, we had a break, free time. My routine is to have a nap in the afternoon – it's one of the core tenets of the Ladies' League of Health and Beauty. They advise twenty minutes, but will tolerate twenty-five.'

Daphne's fingers were now rather numb, her legs she knew were dappled with goose pimples.

'I woke up after about fifteen minutes, though, on account of the shouting,' Irene said matter-of-factly.

'Shouting?' Daphne asked, her excitement thinly veiled. Now they were getting somewhere.

'Robert's dressing room is next to mine – it was him and George, arguing. I couldn't hear everything, even with my ear against the wall. But I did hear Robert tell George, "He mustn't know. I'll get you the money." He said that a couple of times. "He mustn't know."'

'Who? Who mustn't know? And what mustn't he know?' Daphne jabbed her pen at the page in frustration.

'Absolutely no idea, I'm afraid,' Irene said blithely. She shrugged. 'That's all I heard. Struck me as . . . something though.'

It certainly was something, Daphne thought. She sat for a moment, mulling over everything Irene had said. She needed to walk again. Urgently.

'Thank you, Irene, this has all been extremely useful,' she said, standing up. Scurrying away, Daphne turned her attention inwards, to the various thoughts that were tussling with each other in her mind.

The disagreement between George and Robert meant something, she was sure of it. *He mustn't know. I'll get you the money.* Was George blackmailing Robert? What was Robert hiding? George had uncovered some indiscretion of Robert's, undoubtedly. But who did Robert want to keep in the dark? Could Chester have been the *he*? Or was there another *he*?

She stopped. She was going round in circles. Irene's words were just that. While useful, to depend entirely upon those words would be to build her house upon a foundation of sand. No, she needed something firmer, more tangible. Something she could hold on to. She had to return to the hotel bar.

16

Her heart sinking when she realised that the pianist was midway through a mournful rendition of 'Silent Night', Daphne found that a newcomer had arrived at the bar in her absence. Veronica was in conversation with another woman, a woman that Daphne had not met on her whirl-wind tour of the theatre earlier on. She wore her curly black hair, which was salted with white flecks, in an almost defiantly unfashionable style, and her appearance – string of pearls over a black blouse, dark-tinted glasses, black lace gloves – positioned her somewhere between eccentric millionaire widow and reclusive French artist.

Veronica beckoned Daphne over, who, as she approached, adjusted her glasses and removed her coat.

'Daphne, shocker of a day. Where's your drink?' Veronica said. 'Actually, hang on – you must meet Lilian Rogers before you do anything else. Lilian, meet Daphne King of the *Chronicle*.'

'Well, well, a member of the press pack eh,' came the

sardonic reply. 'Are we speaking on or off the record, Miss King?'

'Oh Daphne's never off the clock, Lilian,' Veronica interjected with a wink. 'Daphne, Lilian is a theatrical agent, knows all sorts about who's who and what's what.'

'What a glamorous life you must lead, Lilian. I imagine it's parties and premieres and swanky lunches, day in and day out?' Daphne asked, taking a sip of the red wine which had appeared in her hand. Alfred again.

'Do you know any vets, Daphne?' Lilian Rogers replied after a momentary pause, during which she removed her black gloves for the first time that evening.

Perplexed, Daphne shook her head.

'I do. Vets, Daphne, spend all their waking hours tending to animals. Caring for the lame, responding to the whining, bandaging the bruises,' Lilian said, her face a picture of irony. 'Ask a vet why they do it, and they will tell you that it is their calling. Ask a vet whether they have any pets at home, and ninety per cent of the time they will laugh in your face and say that only a fool would invest time, money and affection in keeping an unpredictable, financially and emotionally draining animal.'

'Right, I see,' Daphne replied, beginning to see where

this vivid portrait of the veterinary profession was heading.

'I am a theatrical agent, Daphne, but I see myself as a vet in many ways: I mop up messes; I tend to injuries that are more often than not self-inflicted; I ensure that my wards are conveyed through their lives in comfort, security and with minimal input into any decisions made on their behalf.' Lilian's pleasure with her analogy was evident as she continued. 'Parties and premieres are to me as limb amputations and catheterisations are to vets: unavoidable operations that require finesse and skill, but which leave me drained and from which I derive very little pleasure.'

With that, she waved her empty wine glass at Donald, prompting him to refill it.

'An inveterate wag is Lilian.' Veronica had clambered out of her seat and was crouching beside Daphne and Lilian. 'She's been in this game for longer than I've been out of short trousers. Nobody stays for that long unless they truly love it. And Lilian truly does. Ask anyone.'

Lilian Rogers was famed – or notorious – throughout Theatreland for many things. In a landscape dominated by men who had played fives against each other at public school before reciting iambic pentameters together at RADA, Lilian stood out like a defiantly sore thumb.

Her life was a true tale of rags to riches that she revelled in. Famously, her mother had been a maid at a country house somewhere in Buckinghamshire and had taken up with the gardener. Young lovers in service, ambition took them to London, where her father had died tragically prematurely, leaving Lilian's mother heartbroken and alone, working in a laundry day and night. Then – as is almost inevitable in such stories – her mother had died when Lilian was fifteen or so, leaving her brother to bring her up. As an apprentice seamstress Lilian had worked on theatrical costumes and her love of theatre was born. Through sheer grit and charisma, and in the face of condescension and resentment from the old-boy network that dominated the West End, she established her own talent agency at the age of twenty-three and became a force to be reckoned with.

Lilian listened to Veronica's nigh-on hagiographical biography before explaining, 'I'm a businesswoman, and I know my business back to front. I also know my reputation for being ruthless. To be frank, it's a reputation that I've cultivated from the off. I see my actors for what they are, and I make sure they get the very best that they can. There's no mysticism or sentimentality: I simply do my job, and I do it well.'

Daphne was in awe. Veronica laughed. 'Lilian, you've struck her dumb. Someone fetch the smelling salts!'

Flushing, Daphne cast a glance over at Donald, Irene and Cecil, all still deep in a hushed conversation.

'So you, er, represent all three of them?' she asked.

Only Donald and Irene apparently. 'Cecil was pulled from the swamp of some am-dram group somewhere – at Robert's insistence. He'd seen him in some humdrum show or other. Woking, was it, Veronica? I forget. Decent enough actor, I'll grant, but doesn't have the chops to go all the way.'

Veronica agreed, 'Far too nice a boy to do the necessary trampling of competitors, not enough cunning to climb the greasy pole. Sends all his earnings back to his mother in wherever-it-is – that's what Alfred told me.'

'An honest actor is as rare as an honest journalist, wouldn't you agree, Miss King?' Lilian smirked, her expression a discombobulating hybrid of playfulness and scorn.

'Speaking of rare breeds, here's one that, let us pray, will be extinct soon.' Veronica rose to her feet, and the party, such as it was, all turned towards a figure who had skulked into the bar.

Short and squat, a man of around sixty stood before them. Glassy eyes a touch too prominent, strands of wispy hair sprouting from his head, he was a striking figure. A grin was plastered on his face, revealing misshapen teeth stained an unbecoming yellow. Had one asked a child to draw a fairy-tale villain in the form of a wicked toad transposed into human form, this might well have been the resulting crayon drawing. And never had Daphne clapped eyes on someone who looked quite so pleased with himself. Donald Hartforth's self-absorption was one thing, but this man oozed the smugness of one steadfast in the belief that he, and he alone, was in possession of the greatest wit and intellect in any room.

'I heard tell there was a little party going on,' the man said, his voice as slimy and unappealing as his visage. 'How perfectly scandalous!'

Tyrone Bridge, bastion of London's theatrical criticism, snaked his way towards the cluster of tables and chairs. 'Hope you don't mind my dropping in; it's a perpetual source of disappointment to me that I can't be at *every* party, but I do pride myself on sniffing out the good ones. And this is simply irresistible: cast assembled to mourn the death of their dearly departed colleague.'

He removed his black coat, laying it delicately on the back of a chair. He wore a yellow bow tie over which his numerous chins wobbled, and he unbuttoned his waistcoat as he helped himself to a glass of wine.

'You swine, you wretched little man.' Donald Hartforth had leaped to his feet and through gritted teeth said, 'I've a mind to give you a going-over, you muckraking hack.'

In a stage whisper Lilian explained to Daphne, 'Dear Donald doesn't enjoy Tyrone's work. His is not a temperament to accept even the gentlest criticism with good grace. And Tyrone certainly doesn't go in for *gentle* criticism. Hasn't had a kind word to say about Donald since he started.'

'Oh dear, oh dear, Donnie,' Bridge trilled in a sing-song voice. 'Still a little sore, are we? Don't worry, you'll be terribly pleased with my musings on the debacles plaguing this production. Managed to file it in record time. Do make sure you pick up a copy in the morning.'

'Don't. Call. Me. DONNIE!' Donald's fist hammered down on the table with a force that shocked even him. As he retook his seat he muttered, 'You're a pathetic little man without a creative bone in you. Be on your way.'

'Donald, come come,' Lilian broke in. 'You're not challenging him to a duel, nor is this a Wild West saloon. Let him have a drink and calm down.'

Daphne took a moment to survey the scene. Catty infighting, repartee, insinuations. All terribly dramatic and witty, but trivial window dressing. She mustn't allow herself to be distracted from the matter at hand. She was not here to let her hair down; she was here to observe, to learn, to decipher and to interpret.

'So the general hypothesis, folks. We're thinking he was bumped off, yes?' Tyrone was asking nobody in particular.

Alfred, shifting uncomfortably in his seat, nodded. 'Looks to be that, yes.'

Tyrone scoffed. 'Well, how immensely convenient for Donnie over there – stepping into the leading man's shoes now, I dare say?'

'They ought to – *hic* – have been his in the first place,' Irene piped, the wine swilling in her glass as she hic-coughed. 'Kept telling him, Donald, it'll all – *hic* – fall into place, didn't I, Donald? Well, that old bacon's well and truly boiled now!'

'Come again?' Alfred asked, his discomfort evolving into distaste.

'Nothing. She's tiddly – ignore her,' Donald snapped. 'Let's get you back to the hotel, Irene, you silly thing.'

'And of course frightfully *in*convenient for Chester,' Tyrone continued, as though Irene's outburst had passed him by entirely. 'Who else will keep all of Chester's secrets now that his right-hand man extraordinaire has croaked? What a pickle he'll be in next time one of his, ahem, indiscretions comes knocking? On the other hand, if one were inclined, one could see it as rather con-venient: Robert Stirling, receptacle of goodness knows what secrets, dead and buried, taking them to his grave.'

Now this was the kind of intelligence that Daphne had been hoping for when she had decided to continue the evening rather than return home.

'Indiscretions, you say?' Daphne repeated encouragingly. In her experience, men like this needed only the slightest of nudges in order to spill a tremendous quantity of beans.

'Oh yes. That pair of dandies, tsk, tsk. The stories one could tell about the hearts they've broken,' Tyrone was trilling. 'Of course, my memoirs – which are bubbling away nicely, thank you very much – will feature the juiciest bits. From those halcyon days when Chester and Robert were just one more pair of bounders in thrall to the elusive whiff of success and the promise of a pretty girl. Or several.'

'Now, now Tyrone,' Lilian said, sighing. 'Please keep your salacious tongue in check – you're in the presence of ladies.'

'Very well, Madame Rogers. Your wish is my command,' Tyrone said gleefully, bowing his head in Lilian's direction. He mimed zipping his mouth closed. 'Mum's the word. My lips are sealed.'

'Oh no need to go that far, Tyrone,' Lilian replied. 'Just please confine yourself to gossip from this decade. I'm sure that our guest here hasn't the slightest interest in your revelations about who spilled whose drink in the Phoenix bar back in the 1910s.'

'Ah, the Phoenix. That's where Chester did all of his early writing – always scribbling away. And more of course. If only those grotty old walls could talk. They'd tell tales that would make your hair curl. Though I see from your current . . . style, Lilian, that you may already have heard your fair share of sordid stories.' Tyrone waggled his eyebrows.

'Theatre critic, gossip-monger, ladies' styling Svengali . . . is there no end to your talents, Tyrone?' Lilian said. 'Pity you were ousted from the inner circle all those years ago. Still have your knickers in a twist after Chester and Robert decided they didn't want to play with poor little Tyrone any more.'

'Ooh, gossip!' Alfred spluttered, evidently having helped himself to rather too much of the red wine. 'Does that mean that you're the one who's been sending those nasty little presents to Chester, Mr Bridge?'

'I beg your pardon?' Tyrone's curiosity was piqued.

Before Daphne could stop him, Alfred trilled, 'Oh yes, some crank's been sending Chester some rather queer gifts. Cigars, wine, a rather gorgeous pen . . .'

'A pen?' Tyrone repeated, his eyes narrowing.

Daphne, aware that Alfred was in danger of letting a

rather valuable cat out of the bag in the presence of a man whose trustworthiness was questionable at best, steered him away from Tyrone back towards Cecil.

Soon conversation moved on to less contentious subjects. She heard Alfred tell Cecil about a revelatory experience he'd had in the presence of a Velazquez in the Prado while on his grand European tour the previous summer. Lilian was explaining to Veronica that, yes, a nine-hour play would be difficult to stage, but it would by no means be impossible. Donald was plying Irene with tap water, a sour look upon his face as he glowered at Tyrone Bridge.

Daphne, through it all, pondered. Pondered Robert's death, pondered that peculiar pen, pondered how on earth it had come to pass that here she was, Daphne King, in a hotel bar drinking red wine at half past ten on a Wednesday night, three days before Christmas.

17

The sliver of light was pitiless. Stabbing her forehead, it was as implacable as it was unwelcome. Daphne had closed the curtains last night in a slipshod fashion, and was rueing her haste now, as she lay in bed, her eider-down and bedspread pulled as high as possible. The sunlight was hell-bent on piercing her cocoon, and, pris-ing one heavy eye open, she saw the ray of light not dancing with but rather charging through the particles of dust hanging in the air.

A groan escaped her as she attempted to roll on to her side to get a better view of the alarm clock that would ordinarily wake her at seven sharp. Five to six? What the blazes was she doing awake at five to six?

Aggrieved and astounded, cheated of a decent night's sleep by her own throbbing head, Daphne groaned again. Hurling the bedclothes away petulantly, she sat upright. Red wine had never agreed with her; it had positively gone out of its way to pick fights with her in fact, and here she was, bearing the consequences. She hauled herself out of bed, tottering towards the window. Tentatively, she peeped through the curtains to find that the white blanket had not melted. *Splendid*. Not only would she have to contend with a raging headache, she would also be battling through inches of snow. She turned to the Christmas cards standing on her desk and, as if revenging herself on the festive season, knocked them down with a swift flick of her hand.

'Daphne, what a horrible little fool you've made of yourself,' she muttered as she turned to assess her face in the mirror that hung on the wall. The dark circles under her eyes were like a scarlet brand, marking her out as a woman who had imbibed far too much wine on a Wednesday night. At least, she reflected, she hadn't said anything wildly inappropriate or behaved in too unprofessional a manner. Reassuring herself, she concluded that, all in all, the evening – the night – had been a fruitful reconnaissance of Theatreland. Perhaps she could reframe the piece with Martin Halliday as a sort of immersive dive into the world of late-night Soho wine escapades. She shook her head. If she were to make her name as a serious journalist, she really mustn't start by telling tales about her own lack of restraint and predilection for cheap red wine.

A knock at the door came.

'One moment, Mrs Booth,' Daphne called in a voice she attempted to infuse with brightness.

'Telephone for you, Miss King,' came the reply.

Telephone? Most likely her mother, wanting to hear which train she was getting today. She groaned yet again. She couldn't go back to Slough today, not when she was just getting started. And certainly not with a headache like this. Daphne scrambled for some clothes, throwing them on and pushing back the waves of nausea which were attempting to sweep her away. A final look in the mirror confirmed that, yes, she did look a fright. So much of a fright that the application of cosmetics would be a fool's errand. Half-heartedly convincing herself that she was ready to face the world, she opened the bedroom door.

There stood Mrs Booth, lavender blouse and pleated skirt just so. A reserved woman given to none of the fripperies that characterised other boarding houses (no porcelain dogs or crocheted cushions to be found under Mrs Booth's roof), she was a fair and decent landlady who lived by one immovable rule: *Don't give me any trouble, and I shan't give you none.* While Daphne had largely managed to keep on the right side of Mrs Booth, she always felt she was traversing a tightrope with her. One false move, and a plummet to an unpleasant doom would result.

'Thank you, Mrs Booth,' Daphne said, trotting briskly down the stairs and taking the phone from where Mrs Booth had left it lying on its table. 'Daphne King speaking?'

'Ah, Miss King,' came a slithering voice dripping with self-satisfaction. 'I do hope I haven't woken you.'

'Tyrone? Mr Bridge?' What the devil was that toad doing calling her at this hour in the morning? And more to the point, how on earth did he know her address or phone number? 'What er . . . what I can do for you?'

'I believe it's more a case of what I can do for you, Miss King. I have some information that I suspect you'll be rather keen to hear. Pertaining to . . . recent matters. Specifically, that pen your squiffy friend mentioned last night. Meet me at the theatre this afternoon – say four o'clock?'

With that, he hung up before Daphne could answer. Curiouser and curiouser.

18

The bus ride from Camberwell to central London had been a journey of peaks and troughs – predominantly troughs of extreme queasiness – but Daphne had endured them with a stoical fortitude. Nevertheless, she had got off the bus early, at Trafalgar Square, so that she could regain her equilibrium.

Passing a newspaper kiosk, she remembered Tyrone Bridge remarking – or rather gloating to Donald – that he had written a piece about the events of the day. Ignoring the front-page headline (WEST END ACTOR DIES onstage), she flicked through the *Standard* impatiently until she reached page 17. Scanning the article, she felt herself wincing. Tyrone had packed no punches. It was a distasteful and crude reflection on Robert's death and the fate of the production now that its leading man was no more. Tyrone took particular delight in lampooning Donald Hartforth. Jokes abounded along the general lines of 'if the show does go on, there will of course still be a stiff corpse cluttering up the stage, that of Donald Hartforth attempting to act' and 'Donald Hartforth's career surely has as much life in it as Robert Stirling's now.' Crass and ill-judged, the cardinal sin of the jokes was, to Daphne's mind, that they simply weren't funny. Wordplay and punning were her stock in trade as Dear Susan, and these quips, such as they were, wouldn't cut the mustard in her column.

Daphne quickened to a half-dash as she made her way towards the theatre. The sunlight which had so indecorously invaded her room earlier was now a welcome companion as she strode past Trafalgar Square, slush beneath her feet. In her mind, Daphne was busy aligning her thoughts, her questions for the day.

As she marched at double speed down Shaftesbury Avenue, she saw ahead the hoarding for the theatre, Robert's cavernous face looming down in all its humbugging glory. She felt a pang of melancholy. No time to stew; there was work to do.

Daphne took a deep breath of the cold air. *Compose yourself, Daphne. It is the 23rd of December 1935, and today you are going to get to the bottom of all of this grubby business.* She greeted Nigel cordially, but found her way blocked by a young police officer.

''Fraid you can't come in here, madam – police

matter,' the constable intoned, his eyes fixed on a point somewhere high above Daphne's head.

'I think you'll find that I am permitted entry; I know Inspector Marklow,' Daphne stated. It was, she feared, futile. The bobby guarding the stage door was far less amenable than old Nigel. Stony-faced and unblinking, his refusal to listen to Daphne was vexatious in the extreme.

'Look here, if you don't let me through, it's going to be one in the eye for you.' She had tried calm reasoning and desperate pleading, if only briefly; now it was the turn of baseless threats. 'I take it that you intend to remain in the force for some time, yes? Well, sonny, you'd best start thinking very carefully about who your friends are. Inspector Marklow is a powerful friend, let me tell you. I certainly wouldn't want—'

'Daphne, you're making a scene,' Marklow sighed as he approached Daphne.

'See!' Daphne pointed a triumphant finger at the stony-faced constable. 'Why hello, Inspector Marklow. How lovely to see you. Kindly tell this young man to allow me to pass.'

Marklow rolled his eyes in the direction of the constable, provoking the tiniest glimmer of a smirk on the young man's hitherto unyielding face.

As he stepped aside to let them through, Daphne

muttered her thanks to the inspector. She had already decided the points that she needed to deal with during this trip, and set about addressing them immediately.

'I'm just here to pop to the dressing rooms. New friend of mine, Veronica, she's left . . . something there. Said I'd get it for her.'

'Very well, Daphne. Can't be standing in the way of Miss Daphne King on a mission to retrieve . . . something.'

Nodding in what she hoped was an authoritative manner at the numerous police officers she passed on her way, Daphne headed directly for her intended destination: Chester's dressing room. The door was ajar, and she closed it behind her as she stepped inside.

The bouquets were on the turn now, a slight odour of stagnant water detectable. A few petals had fallen, littering the carpet.

In the corner was the safe. Within it lay the pen that Chester had received. She was certain that if she could examine it, she might alight upon a telling detail, a significant clue that would lead to enlightenment.

She crouched down in front of it and retrieved a kirby grip from her satchel. The Girl Guides had been a trial and a bore, with the exception of the one morning they had spent on survival and escape skills. They had had a guest to lead this session, and Daphne had been dismayed to learn afterwards that the woman had not been invited back. Despite being called Dottie, she was a serious, no-nonsense adventurer whose expeditions had taken her to Ben Nevis, the Himalayas and the forests of Bavaria. Dottie had imparted innumerable tips that morning back in 1911, primarily on the subject of how to repurpose domestic utensils if one found oneself in a sticky situation. The powers that be had afterwards decided that picking locks was, rather than an essential survival skill, more readily classified as a tool for juvenile delinquency.

Daphne thought of Dottie as she picked the lock on the safe. *Gently, gently, easy does it*. And *voilà*! The telltale click of the cogs, and the door swung open.

Daphne peered inside. This couldn't be right. There was no pen. Just the biscuit tin she had noticed beside the mirrors yesterday. Had Chester taken the pen with him to the hotel after all? She felt around inside the safe, just in case she had missed it. No, it was decidedly free from pens. This made her even more certain that the pen signified *something*.

She fished out the biscuit tin. Surely Chester didn't prize his garibaldis this highly.

Daphne took the tin and sat on the chaise longue. It was battered, the lettering on the top of the lid scratched and faded. Opening it, hoping for the pen,

Daphne braced herself for what else she might find. Illicit love letters? Blackmail demands? Scandalous photographs?

Inside was a small bundle of postcards. She leafed through them – seaside scenes from Blackpool, Scarborough, Brighton and Margate. Turning each one over, she was puzzled to find that, in lieu of a wish-you-were-here message, every card bore but one sentence. Epigrammatic and cryptic. She took out her notebook and transcribed the lines carefully for later review far from the risk of a police constable blundering in.

She returned the postcards to the tin, and, on so doing, she noticed another item within it. It was a photograph, curling at the edges. She extracted it and examined it closely.

A scribbled date in the corner placed it in 1912, twenty-three years ago. It was a portrait of a small group in a pub, a scene of conviviality and bonhomie. There were four figures in the foreground, their backs to the bar. Daphne's eyes were drawn immediately to the central figure: Robert Stirling. He must have been, in this moment crystallised by a Kodak camera, around his mid-thirties. A pint of beer in one hand, he was leaning back against the bar, his face mirthful. Next to him, in a similar position, was Chester Harrison. Even then his beard was notable for its lustre, and the mischief in his eyes was even more pronounced. With one hand he was clutching a glass while his other arm was draped around the waist of a smiling young woman. Theodora? Daphne peered at the woman. Although undoubtedly beautiful – her hair piled atop her head in the fashion of the day, a silver choker around her neck – she was not Theodora. Daphne frowned before peering at the fourth figure. Standing to Robert's right, a grin plastered across his face, it took Daphne a moment to place him. Not because the intervening decades had altered his appearance significantly; no, his bulging eyes and heavyset middle she recognised in a heartbeat. No, Daphne had trouble placing him purely because of her initial disbelief. There was Tyrone Bridge, arm in arm with Robert Stirling. Chester and Robert and Tyrone.

She had known that Chester and Robert had been friends for decades, and she had been apprised of the fact that, back in the depths of history, Tyrone had counted himself their friend as well. Yet seeing them together as younger men was something of a jolt. The photograph was from a time before Chester became a successful director, when he was still muddling through with middling Shakespearean productions. Before Tyrone's wicked wit had the power to demolish or elevate careers. Before Robert was . . . well, dead.

Daphne peered once more at the young woman. Was

there something in her eyes that she recognised? A shadow to her smile that was familiar?

She turned the photograph over and immediately chided herself for not doing so earlier, for there was a note written on the back:

July 1912 – Opening night, A Midsummer
   Night's Dream

Dearest Robert,

A souvenir of our time together.
Kisses and love from your darling girl,

Josie

She placed the photograph in her satchel and turned over the postcards once again. No indication of the sender, nothing distinctive that might nudge her in one direction or another. Although ... hello ... what was this? None of the postcards except one – the one depicting a scene from Brighton – bore a postmark. It hadn't been hand-delivered but posted. And there, just there, was the postmark: Little Grinton. She hadn't the foggiest where Little Grinton was, but Daphne would find out and get there today, by hook or by crook.

She slipped the postcard from Little Grinton into her

satchel next to the photograph, questions swimming – or rather thrashing and gulping for air and eventually sinking – in Daphne's mind. The woman in the photograph was a sweetheart of Robert's? 'Kisses and love' would suggest so. The arm around the waist supported that. Could it be that there was some connection between this woman and Robert's death? Were the postcards reminders to Robert and Chester? Had this Josie been one of Robert's wronged women? They had all clearly been acquainted with her. Daphne attempted to piece it all together, but it was as though two entirely different puzzles had been carelessly shoved into the same box. Some pieces refused to fit together, and many were missing.

She could hear a police officer bellowing incoherently in the corridor. She bit her lip, her conscience muttering at her, *Give the tin to Marklow. He's a detective, a man whose very lifeblood is the solving of crimes and the piecing together of clues. Hand it over to him, tell him about the pranks, the arguments.*

Daphne's conscience was a tiresome nag. An absent-minded nag at that, for it had evidently forgotten that snake Jamie Jenkins and his habit of snaffling her leads and claiming all the glory. He had suffered no pangs of conscience when stealing her work, so why on earth should she listen to hers?

Her instinct and her ambition were, on this occasion,

a far more appealing chorus: *Take the tin, keep the photograph, follow your nose.* This tin was the key to it all; she knew it. If she could only have more time, she was sure she could unlock everything. It all led back to Chester, Robert, Tyrone, the 'old gang'.

Her decision made, the tin joined her other discoveries in her satchel. This moment was, she reflected later, the point of no return. She was no longer docile Dear Susan, nor could she ever return to being her. Being forthright in her questions and assertions was one thing, but this – secreting away a piece of evidence, *stealing* a piece of evidence – well, this was quite another. Daphne was acutely aware that, were her instincts wrong, she could well be heading not towards glory and justice, but ignominy and no job. Yet she felt a certainty that her instincts were far from wrong.

19

Bursting through the doors to the Regency a short while later, Daphne was met once more with the lacklustre tinkling of the piano. This time, the residents of the hotel were being treated to a dour rendition of 'O Come All Ye Faithful' as they tucked into their breakfasts. She dashed into the dining room, eyes scanning around. She needed to speak to Veronica, share her findings with someone in possession of a clear mind and a frank opinion.

'Oh hello, Daphne. 'Fraid nobody else is awake yet. Anything I can do?'

Daphne found herself in the full beam of an open, frank smile from Cecil Milford, who was sitting at a small table. His white shirt tucked neatly into grey flannel trousers, golden hair parted in a precise clean line, face unblemished, he showed no sign that he too had been in the theatre bar until an ungodly hour last night.

'Cecil, you look as fresh as a daisy! I, meanwhile, could very much be mistaken for someone on the brink of pushing up the daisies,' Daphne wittered, before realising that wordplay relating to euphemisms for death might be construed as misjudged at best, tasteless at worst. She glanced at her watch. Quarter past nine. It was rather early. But there was much to be done. 'I'll . . . I'll wait here for Veronica.'

Cecil suggested that she take a seat at his table, and so it was that Daphne King found herself drinking a bitter black coffee opposite an absurdly handsome young man. Am-dram in Woking, was that what Lilian Rogers had told her last night? Cecil looked to be no older than twenty-two, so extraordinarily lucky to be plucked from obscurity and deposited on the West End stage by such prestigious figures as Chester Harrison and Theodora D'Arby.

'Family out in Woking, is that right?' Daphne asked. Although she had far more pressing matters to be attending to, a touch of small talk wouldn't go amiss.

'Just me and my mum, yes,' Cecil replied, his eyes catching the light in a most becoming way. 'She's always been very supportive, really good to me. Worked ever so hard to help me. Don't know where I'd be without her.'

'Hmm, that's very nice,' Daphne remarked, listlessly stirring her coffee. 'And what is it your mother does?'

'Well, just now she's poorly,' he answered, his voice

quavering slightly. 'She's had a bit of a tough time of it, in all honesty.'

Daphne noted a shift in Cecil's tone. No longer was he merely humouring her attempts at chit-chat; he seemed to want to *share* something with her.

'A tough time how, exactly?' Daphne asked encouragingly.

'Life, I suppose you might say,' Cecil replied bluntly.

'I see,' Daphne said. Though she didn't see quite yet. Some truth was hovering just out of reach.

'Sorry, Miss King, you must find this rather irksome. You barely know me, yet here I am, telling you all about my mother first thing in the morning.' Cecil gave a wistful smile. 'It's just . . . well, I don't get the chance to speak to many people. Alfred's been a pal, a real pal – don't get me wrong – it's just that . . . well, it's nice to have someone else to talk to.'

Oh Lord, thought Daphne. Handsome, lonely, sensitive. Next he'd be informing her that he spent his free time rescuing kittens from trees.

'Alfred's been showing me the ropes with some painting, as it happens,' Cecil continued. 'Only a spot of still life, nothing too modern or . . . risqué, mind. Acting can be . . . quite draining. I've enjoyed the, as they say, quiet contemplation offered by painting.'

'Oh crikey, well, quiet contemplation is something

we could all do with a bit more of these days, I should say.' Daphne chuckled. 'Wouldn't it be divine to take a promenade around the Royal Academy right now? Rather than ...' She gestured around the threadbare dining room.

At this, Cecil brightened, shaking off a little of the melancholy that the discussion of his mother seemed to have engendered.

'I can't offer you a trip to the RA, Miss King – not sure I've time today – but I do have some of my paintings upstairs in my room. If you'd care to have a look? Perhaps you can offer me some constructive criticism?'

If Daphne wasn't very much mistaken, this young man was flirting with her. Heavens to Betsy. This certainly wouldn't do. She needed to speak to Veronica. But then again, where was the harm in humouring the chap – taking a glance at his paintings?

Wincing through a final mouthful of coffee – bitter though it was, she was in dire need of caffeine this morning – she tucked in her chair and followed the dashing Mr Milford up to his room – the decor of which was, as she discovered upon entering, as bland and unremarkable as the bar and dining room downstairs.

Cecil set about rummaging through a pile of canvases underneath the window, amiably wittering about whether he ought to show her the oranges or the apples; the oranges were from his early dabblings, the apples a later work. Or perhaps it would be better to share his flower series?

As Cecil mulled over his options, Daphne surveyed the unrelenting sea of beige which consumed the room and all the furnishings within it. The bed was made up, not a wrinkle in the coverlet, while on the bedside table she saw a paperback copy of *Great Expectations.*

An open wardrobe door displayed Cecil's clothes, every item immaculately pressed and hanging neatly. A mirror, a small chip in one corner, hung above a table upon which Cecil's cosmetics lay – pomade, some cologne.

Inside the frame of the mirror, she noticed, Cecil had lodged a small photograph. She took a step closer to peer at it: a young woman was clutching a small boy as they both sat cross-legged underneath a Christmas tree, wide happy smiles upon both of their faces.

'A little keepsake that Mum sent me – she's missing me.' Cecil had glanced up and seen Daphne looking at the photo. 'A reminder of a Christmas from when I was little – to make sure I go home this year!'

While at the table downstairs Daphne had been able to produce suitable responses to such conversational gambits, this time she found herself unable to respond, for she was peering intently at the photograph, raising a hand to her mouth. The photograph showed the same beaming woman she had seen before – nestling in between Robert and Chester in another photograph. The photograph she had found in Chester's safe.

The woman – Josie – was Cecil's mother.

20

A man dressed as Father Christmas had stationed him-self in the square outside, and was clanging a bell rather tiresomely. 'I've half a mind to knock him on the head with that infernal thing,' Daphne grumbled, pacing back and forth in another beige hotel room, this one occupied by Veronica Burford.

'Now, now, Daphne,' Veronica enjoined calmly, 'let's not have you carted off for assault and battery of Saint Nick. The matter at hand, if you please. You were saying?'

'I just . . . It can't be a bloody coincidence!' Daphne exclaimed. 'Of course, yes, at a push I could be per-suaded to believe in a certain degree of serendipity in the universe. Arriving at the station late only to find that one's train has been fortunately delayed anyway; discovering that one's purse is at home, but finding a ten-shilling note in one's pocket. That sort of thing. But to come across a decades-old photograph with Chester and Robert cosying up to an attractive woman who just happens to be Cecil Milford's mother – to shrug that off as coincidence would be, to put it kindly, dimwitted.'

'I'll grant you that,' Veronica conceded. 'But I'm not entirely certain what we're to do with this information.'

'Don't you see? Cecil's mother Josie was photographed in 1912 in the arms of Robert Stirling. Robert Stirling has a reputation for womanising. Twenty-three years after the photograph is taken, Robert Stirling swoops in to plonk Cecil Milford on the London stage for no discernible reason.'

'In point of fact, Cecil's a rather good actor,' Veronica interjected.

'Yes, yes, I'm sure he is,' Daphne dismissed. 'But the point is: if Robert Stirling mistreated Cecil's mother . . . well, that's a jolly good reason to want to hurt him, wouldn't you say?'

Veronica frowned and admitted that, yes, there was something in that.

'I'll say!' Daphne was still pacing. 'Now, the question is: what about the postcards?'

In the kerfuffle that had ensued after Daphne had made her excuses, left Cecil's room and banged on Veronica's door, the matter of the postcards had been ignored. Veronica, still clad in her silk black and white pyjamas, guided Daphne to a chair, poured her a glass of water and instructed her to take a deep breath and to share her findings.

'Hmm,' Veronica responded after she had done so, her tone measured and neutral.

'*Hmm? Hmm* is all you have to say?' Daphne spluttered and recommenced her pacing.

'Darling, you really must contain yourself,' Veronica purred.

Daphne faltered and sat back down. 'Oh, it's all a muddle, Veronica.'

'Imagine you're speaking to someone especially dense – a stretch, I know, given my towering intellect – but just imagine I have no idea what the devil is going on. That, I should say, is much less of a stretch,' Veronica said calmly. 'Tell me what we know so far about the postcards, and what we need to do.'

Daphne thought for a moment, the whispers and mutterings within her mind settling themselves into something resembling an orderly list. The inventory of knowns was mounting, now that she could add Cecil Milford's parentage to it – or rather, his presumed parentage. 'If the postcards were hand-delivered, they were delivered by someone close to the company, someone who was at every theatre you stopped at. Except that the person delivering the postcards by hand couldn't go to Brighton. They had a postcard from Brighton, yes, but for some reason our mysterious postcard-sender-slash-courier wasn't actually *in* Brighton to deliver it to the theatre.'

'Something kept our . . . postcard-sender-slash-courier from going to the theatre in Brighton. Illness? Fear of being recognised?' Veronica mused.

'It's immaterial what stopped them from being there,' Daphne said. 'What matters is that they were in Little Grinton. We need to go to Little Grinton.' She glanced at her watch – half past ten. She had to meet Tyrone Bridge at four o'clock. 'Where the bloody hell is Little Grinton?'

'It's an hour outside London, towards Surrey,' Veronica answered.

'All the trains will be playing silly buggers this time of year; Christmas timetables are an absolute farce. Fat chance of catching one today,' Daphne was pacing again. 'Unless . . . You don't have an automobile, do you, Veronica?'

A smile crept across Veronica's face. 'Alas no, but I know an obliging gentleman who does.'

21

'You'd better write a fiendishly good piece about me after this, King,' Donald Hartforth blared over the engine as he took yet another corner rather too quickly for Daphne's liking. It required a tremendous force of will to stop her imagining them screeching to gruesome deaths courtesy of a patch of black ice.

It had been a test to cajole Donald into helping them, but Veronica had evidently refined her tactics: a smattering of flattery, a soupçon of flirtation, a dash or two of empty promises and hey presto!

In this case, the empty promises had been vivid descriptions of the flattering profile that Daphne would write of him: full page, two – possibly three – photographs of Donald (final approval his, naturally), some fawning prose about his soon-to-be-starring role as Scrooge.

'Absolute travesty that I wasn't given top billing in the first place. I know Robert's dead, but he was a godawful actor. Heaven knows why I let Lilian coax me into playing second fiddle to a humdrum has-been,' he barked. 'Although that rather does has-beens a disservice. Robert Stirling was more a, how shall we say, never-was-in-the-first-place.'

'Donald, if you're going to go on like this the entire trip, we'll boot you out and take the car ourselves – never mind our collective lack of licence or prior experience,' Veronica said from the back seat.

'So how *did* she coax you?' Daphne asked, eager to extract as much information from Donald as possible. She wasn't in this car for the sheer fun of it; this was in the cause of her professional duties.

'Come again?' Donald replied, irritated that Daphne was attempting to steer him away from his favourite topic: his talent, and the lack thereof in his peers.

'Lilian, your agent – how did she coax you into doing this play?'

'Oh, some stuff and nonsense about Chester being a living legend, Theodora being a magnet for publicity. Convinced me that it would be advantageous for my *profile*. Well, can't say she was wrong, on reflection,' Donald admitted. 'Irene is, as I'm sure you've deduced, less content with her lot in the play. Hobbling about as Tiny Tim hasn't been a terribly effective showcase for her talents, alas.'

'Right! Turn right here, Donald!' Veronica, in her role

as navigator, had the map open on the seat beside her. 'Now we're on the open road, ladies and gentlemen, I think it's about time for a festive singsong – "Twelve Days of Christmas", everyone?'

Daphne groaned. 'Must we, Veronica? I think I'd rather discuss what it is we're going to do once we get to Little Grinton.'

She leaned her head against the window and peered out at the fast-moving wintry landscape outside. If Little Grinton was a busted flush, if this all came to nothing, perhaps she should ask Donald to drop her off in Slough on the way back. What would her mother be doing now, the morning before Christmas Eve? Most likely wrapping up the last of the presents, checking the contents of the larder to ensure that everything had been bought. Her sister Felicity would be arriving in time for lunch. And here Daphne was, hurtling along in a car driven by a theatre actor towards . . . what, precisely? She shook her head. She mustn't be pessimistic; she should trust her instincts. She would unravel this queer business with precision and poise, and she would tell Mother and Felicity all about it in due course.

'Oh Daphne, look at you, all serious,' Veronica began. 'It's perfectly simple: we go to the village post office, enquire after any murderers who've been knocking around waving stolen pens about and throwing poisonous mushrooms at people, then Bob's your uncle, Fanny's your aunt. We blow the case wide open, and we all have some mulled wine back in Soho.'

Daphne smiled. It was all rather ludicrous when put in such a way, she had to admit. 'Very well. *I'll* blow the case wide open, and *you* can be in charge of the mulled wine.'

'Excuse me for intruding on your badinage, ladies, but where does yours truly figure in all this?' Donald asked.

'You'll be tucked up safely in bed, waiting for Father Christmas to deliver your presents, a sparkling, full-page interview in the *Chronicle* dedicated to you, your startling good looks and your otherworldly acting talent,' Daphne replied. For all his pomp and bluster, his self-aggrandisement and narcissism, she was beginning to grow rather fond of Donald Hartforth.

22

Mercifully, Veronica gave up on the singsong after seven swans a-swanning, and they arrived in Little Grinton at just after half past eleven. Flakes had started to fall once again, and the village looked like a snow globe, picturesque and peaceful, a million miles from the hubbub of London.

'Christ alive, this place looks a yawn,' Donald said as he parked his car on what appeared to be the high street. Daphne and Veronica set off, having told Donald to stay in the car – an instruction to which he was all too happy to adhere. 'Be my pleasure, ladies. Don't know what I might catch from these country folk.'

'We're in *Surrey*, Donald, it's hardly the back of beyond,' Daphne grumbled as she shut the car door.

She and Veronica picked their way through the snow, passing a toy shop that promised 'England's most incredible railway set' and 'Latest model of Baby Betty now in – her own real woollen cardigan included!', an antique shop displaying a fetching standard lamp ('We're not here to do our shopping, Veronica'), and a clothes shop whose window boasted woollen mittens in fifty-seven different colours.

Reaching the post office, Daphne was overcome with jitters. What exactly did she hope to achieve here? Did, as Veronica had suggested, she really think that the nice lady who worked there would tell her that, yes, funnily enough, there was a peculiar person in just the other week, chatting all about their plans to murder someone named Robert Stirling. Didn't think anything of it at the time, mind, but now you mention it . . .

Daphne shook her head, dispelling these thoughts. Any clue, any hint as to who had sent the postcard would help them. It was a small village, after all. Whoever it was might be a resident, in which case the post office could lead them directly to the sender.

A rusty bell clanged as they walked through the door. Tinsel was hanging from every conceivable nook and indeed cranny, while a mechanical knee-high Father Christmas rang a bell and bellowed, 'Ho, ho, ho.'

'Season's greetings! How may I help you both today?' came an exceedingly jolly voice from behind the till. The woman wore tinsel about her neck; her rosy cheeks matched her red jumper, and her smile betrayed no sign of cynicism or weariness at having to share a shop with an interminably ho-ho-ho-ing Father Christmas.

Daphne had known it: here *was* the nice lady in the post office.

'Oh hello, I do hope you can,' Daphne began, rummaging in her satchel as she approached the till. Veronica sauntered after her, a smile upon her face, eager to hear what Daphne was going to ask.

'You see . . . I . . . well, I was hoping you might be able to tell me if you remember somebody posting this.' She passed the postcard to the woman, 'From your fine establishment here.'

'Oh lovey, chance'd be a fine thing!' the woman exclaimed. 'I'd love to help you, really I would, but I'd have to have the memory of an elephant to remember who sent a *postcard*. Give me a special delivery bouquet or a telegram to Australia and I might be able to summon it up, but a *postcard*? Well, that's nothing to write home about.' She guffawed at what Daphne could only presume was a post-office in-joke.

'Yes, yes, I suppose that's true enough,' Daphne said, a sigh escaping her. If only it had memorably been sent by a beautiful woman going by the name of Josie Milford, mother to a beautiful son named Cecil Milford and jilted lover of Robert Stirling.

Veronica sidled over. 'Come on, Daphne, we tried. Let's get back to London – mulled wine on me, yes?'

'Oh a lovely drop of mulled wine, lucky you! Though I shall be having my own drop of that for Christmas Eve tomorrow up at Cartley Manor,' the woman said.

'Oh yes?' Daphne asked automatically. 'Is that the local hotel?'

'Lord no!' the woman exclaimed, laughing. 'No, Cartley Manor's the old folks' home. Terribly swish, it is. They have a little do every Christmas Eve – a bit of a dance for the oldies up there. Some of them not so old, mind, just a bit . . . doddery. Lost some of their marbles along the way. We have crackers, mince pies, the lot. They go to their own families for the day itself, of course, but it's a lovely village affair tomorrow.'

'How wonderful,' Veronica replied, Daphne seemingly lost in thought. 'Well, a merry Christmas to you, and make sure you enjoy that mulled wine.'

After Veronica had guided her back into the street, Daphne turned and gripped her shoulders. 'An old folks' home!'

Veronica was puzzled by the outburst.

'Oh Veronica, do keep up,' Daphne exclaimed as she rubbed her gloved hands together and began striding back to the car. 'The postcard was sent from Little Grinton, that much we know. Sent from here because the sender was *here* rather than in Brighton. Every single other postcard was hand-delivered to the theatres.'

'Wait, I think I'm following you . . .'

'The person sending the postcards couldn't make it to Brighton because they were stuck here.'

Veronica trotted to catch up with Daphne, who had set a formidable pace.

'They were here, in Little Grinton. That much is certain. Now, I don't know about you, but I'm not excessively keen on wandering the snowy streets knocking on doors, interrupting families the day before Christmas Eve and asking them if they've been sending strange parcels to Chester Harrison,' Daphne explained. 'I'm assuming the person who sent the postcards also sent the parcels. It's all been carried out painstakingly – every theatre, every venue.'

Veronica nodded in agreement, but her face indicated that she didn't quite follow Daphne's train of thought.

'We have an established pattern: parcels and postcards hand-delivered to every theatre.' Daphne was now speaking slowly. 'When we have an established pattern, any interruption to it, any deviation from it, well, that's what we need to put under the microscope. A pattern isn't broken lightly. It would take something of significance to cause our sender to break their routine. What if the sender was summoned somewhere because of an emergency and wasn't able to get to Brighton?'

'The sender falling ill suddenly ...?' Veronica asked.

Daphne shook her head. 'Possible. But think about it, Veronica. There's no hospital here in Little Grinton. If the sender were poorly enough to not be able to get to Brighton, why would they be in Little Grinton? We know there's an old folks' home here. That is a fact. What if the sender was called to the old folks' home for some urgent reason? What if the sender was visiting someone there?'

'But what if the sender just so happens to *live* here?' Veronica asked, truly embracing the role of devil's advocate as they traipsed through the snow.

'Oh, you *are* an infuriating creature, Veronica!' Daphne came to an abrupt halt in the street. 'If the sender lives here, we'll have a blasted tough job finding them. If, on the other hand, there's a connection to this Cartley Manor place ... well that's a far easier needle to find in a much more manageable haystack, wouldn't you say?' She grinned at Veronica. 'In lieu of any other certainty here in Little Grinton, surely it's worth checking Cartley Manor? Either eliminating it from our enquiries, or confirming its significance?'

'You're positively *lapping* this up, Daphne!' Veronica replied. 'I fear we're one sleuthing revelation away from you buying a pipe and calling me Watson.'

'You should be so lucky,' Daphne rejoined, before clambering back into the car.

23

Donald Hartforth had encountered plentiful situations of an off-kilter nature. Playing Iago in 1931 (an interpretation in which he unashamedly took on the persona of a strutting pantomime villain), his counterpart playing Othello had insisted on introducing a bizarrely moving ballroom dancing interlude into the handkerchief scene; as a peacocking Mercutio in *Romeo and Juliet* he had been subject to a barrage of ladies' underwear flung at him during curtain calls. He prided himself on welcoming such situations with open arms, for 'If we are not challenging ourselves and being challenged, we are not growing as professionals.'

So it was that he gracefully and unquestioningly nodded his agreement when Daphne King asked him to drive them to an old people's home so that she could attempt to obtain a list of the residents there. Of course. What else did he have to do today?

Cartley Manor, despite its size, was neither imposing

nor grand, but rather a homely and inviting red-brick building of three storeys. Daphne could see that each of its numerous windows had been decorated on the inside with a paper snowflake. Smoke danced from a chimney, and beside the driveway leading to the building itself various shrubs bore what appeared to be home-made Christmas decorations, which, though somewhat soggy due to the weather, still appeared cheerful and deter-mined to inspire a festive spirit: lopsided wooden stars here, oranges spiked with cloves there. A makeshift Nativity scene – garden gnomes standing in for the Three Wise Men, a teddy bear lying in the manger – greeted the car as it approached, while a distinct aroma of baking gingerbread permeated the air. Acres of snow-encased land surrounded the house; a copse sprang from the middle of one field, while a glittering lake shone brightly beyond another.

'Might check myself in here. Rather jolly place,' Veronica said as Donald parked the car. Daphne once again instructed their driver to remain *in situ*, but this time Donald demurred.

'Now, I can't say that I'm entirely clear as to what it is you're up to,' he began, 'but seems to me in a place like this, you can't have too many cooks, because the broth is going to be revolting whatever happens. What say you put my good looks to some use, eh? Daphne, I made a meal of it when Robert died, was absolutely useless – let me make up for it?'

This was the first mention of Donald's failure to act when Robert had died in front of them. Daphne furrowed her brow. Donald Hartforth – a changed man, or so it seemed.

It was agreed that yes, all three would go inside. It was further agreed that no, it was unlikely the staff would be so obliging as to provide Daphne with a list of the residents. Therefore it was thirdly agreed that the three would pose as siblings evaluating the home as a potential destination for their ailing parent.

'Och halloo!' Donald greeted the man behind the desk. 'We'd vey mooch like te speak wit' ye in regards ooor farther, if ye please.'

Daphne and Veronica glanced at each other. It had not been agreed that they were Scottish siblings, but it should have been foreseen that Donald would grasp the limelight with zeal.

The man behind the desk introduced himself as Francis and shook their hands warmly. Shorter than Daphne, he appeared queerly ageless: his benevolent face bore no wrinkles, yet his white hair sprang up in sparse tufts from his head. Behind him stood a magnificent Christmas tree, and Daphne could see a group of elderly residents playing cards at a table beside it. The air was filled with the aroma of hot chocolate and oranges, a scent so enveloping that Daphne suspected it had been created especially to create a cosy ambience.

'My brother here,' Veronica said, glaring at Donald, 'who was born in Scotland, hence his . . . accent, is eager for our father to become a resident at this wonderful establishment. My sister and I, who were both born in *England*, hence *our* accents, are undecided. Might we trouble you for some information?'

Donald scowled at Veronica's unwillingness to play along. 'Yeees, wair keen to nooo hooo thay spend thair days.'

Daphne winced and hoped that Francis didn't have any Scottish cousins or close friends; if he did, he would surely be perplexed as to the provenance of this particular accent. As Francis began dutifully and enthusiastically outlining the daily routine at Cartley Manor, Daphne's eyes wandered to the ledger upon which his hands rested. It bore signatures and dates – a visitors' book. *Aha*.

'Perhaps you might take us on a tour, Francis?' Daphne asked brightly.

Francis puckered his lips. 'Now that might be a little tricky; it being so close to Christmas, we're slightly low on staff – nothing that puts us in a pickle, of course, but it does mean that I'm unable to leave the desk. The telephone might ring, a visitor might arrive – you understand, I'm sure.'

Daphne's smile faltered. 'Of course, of course we understand.'

'Perhaps my brother and I can take a turn?' Veronica gestured vaguely behind Francis, to where the card game was in full swing. 'We won't stray where you can't see us. It would just be wonderful to, well, soak up the atmosphere a little. I believe that my sister has further questions, so perhaps she can stay here with you?'

Veronica's bulging eyes and jerking head movements indicated to Daphne that a plot was afoot; they indicated to Francis that this strange woman was exceptionally keen to take a turn. Agreeing, he returned his attention to Daphne.

'How else may I help you?' he asked.

'Ah, yes ... I was ... I was wondering about the grounds – they look delightful. And are the residents permitted to avail themselves of the surrounding countryside?' It was all Daphne could pluck from the ether to ask, but it was a random selection that was to prove exceedingly fortuitous.

'Yes, we're terribly fortunate here at Cartley Manor,' Francis replied. 'The fields surrounding the house are open to residents all year round, and they do so love strolling around. Beautiful views, quite quite stunning. Access to the wood and lake is slightly more restricted; residents are permitted there between the months of March to August, but with supervision by members of staff.'

'Right, right, of course – wouldn't want anyone falling into the lake,' Daphne said, looking to see what the blazes Veronica and Donald were up to.

'Quite, quite. And there are the mushrooms of course. We've had gardeners in, tried everything, but there's no getting rid of them. Eradicate them in one spot, they pop up in another. We've had to cordon off swathes of the wood on account of them.'

'On account of who?' Daphne asked, betraying the minimal attention she'd been paying to poor Francis.

'On account of the mushrooms – the dangerous mushrooms,' he stated matter-of-factly.

Daphne's stomach flipped. She gulped at the air around her. 'I'm so sorry. The dangerous mushrooms?'

A clatter behind Francis prevented him from answering. Peering over his shoulder, Daphne spied Veronica giving her an ostentatious wink. The cards were strewn across the floor, and Donald, along with two extremely elderly residents, were down on their knees attempting to retrieve them.

Francis darted over to assist them, shouting, 'Norman, Norman, off the floor, Norman. You know your knees won't thank you for it.'

Daphne swept around the side of the desk and grabbed the ledger, flipping the pages back to the date from the postcard: seven days ago, December 16th. Her finger on the page, she scanned for any names that she recognised, any that rang a bell however tiny that bell might be. Nothing. Certainly no Milford. *Damn.* The fracas was subsiding and there was only one thing for it: she ripped the page from the ledger and stuffed it in her satchel. Like a greedy mapgie, she was acquiring quite a collection of trinkets: postcards, photograph, now a page torn from Cartley Manor visitors' book. If only she had that blasted pen, she would have a full house of clues to piece together.

'Thank ye soo mooch for yer hailp,' Donald enunciated with painful imprecision as Francis escorted him back to the desk, followed by Veronica. The cards were being shuffled once more, and Norman looked none too pleased about recent events.

'Yes, thank you, Francis,' Daphne added. 'You've been more helpful than you could possibly know.'

Francis beamed at the trio and asked whether it was Dundee or the Isle of Skye that Donald hailed from. Donald was replying that he had in fact been born in the castle of Dunsinane when Daphne interrupted to enquire as to whether she could be a frightful cheek and visit the wood? And if, perhaps, they might be able to borrow some welly-boots?

Veronica glanced at her, throwing a knowing smile her way. There was no way of telling what Daphne King had in mind, but Veronica was willing to bet it would be perfectly delicious.

'Well, no wellies, I'm afraid, but as you do seem rather keen on exploring, I can allow you to go as far as the north side of the wood – they'll have my guts for garters if you're caught near the lake. Ever since Mrs Dundridge told all and sundry it was frequented by mermaids, it's been a nightmare keeping them out of there,' Francis confided.

Daphne led the way outside, an eager Veronica by her side, a reluctant Donald trailing behind. 'Listen here. I'm not one for traipsing through the muck – in a literal sense,' he called as they charged ahead.

'Hush, Donald. Our friend Francis will be wondering where your Scottish brogue has gone,' Daphne urged.

'He's gone back to the car,' Veronica said, her breathing heavy as she tried to keep up with Daphne.

The snow crunching beneath their feet, their shoes quickly becoming sodden, Daphne and Veronica made their way out of the grounds and across a pure white, completely untrodden field. If Daphne hadn't been so fixated on finding the mushrooms, she might have noted the beauty of the scene: the way the December sun, now emerging coyly from behind a cloud, beamed down upon the already dazzling landscape. Veronica, gamely keeping up, said, 'Remind me – how is it that you've come to be a dab hand at identifying fatally poisonous mushrooms?'

'It's the fantastical and varied life of an agony aunt, though I should add that anyone with even a rudimentary understanding of fungi could spot the buggers we're after,' Daphne explained, swerving left into the wood. 'If they're not here . . . well, I might find myself having to eat a hefty slice of humble pie.'

'Having seen you in action today, I rather suspect it won't come to that,' Veronica reassured Daphne, following her into the wood.

It was darker under the trees, with an even more stinging chill in the air. Daphne licked her finger and stuck it aloft. 'This way,' she commanded, heading towards a towering oak tree that stood at the northern perimeter of the wood.

There, at the base of its trunk, nestled among the snow that had managed to penetrate the wood, was a group of tiny white stumps, almost invisible to the casual eye. Daphne hunkered down to examine them.

'That's them, all right,' she whispered, as if forgetting Veronica's presence. 'Not at your biggest and baddest now it's winter. But that's them. That's what killed Robert.'

24

Daphne felt as though they were flying all the way back to London, such was her elation. She had been right: Little Grinton had held the key! Not only the key, but the mushrooms. Here was incontrovertible proof that linked it all: the postcard was from Little Grinton, the mushrooms were from Little Grinton. She was getting closer to the identity of the culprit, the person who had sent the parcels to Chester and who had poisoned Robert.

And in an hour she would be meeting Tyrone Bridge, whose enigmatic telephone call that morning had promised intelligence on that most elusive piece of the jigsaw, the pen. The pen which was now missing.

Although she had attempted to conceal her glee, she couldn't resist telling Veronica and Donald precisely what she had pieced together.

'You clever thing, you,' Veronica said admiringly. Donald remained curiously mute.

'Now I just need to pore over this visitors' book . . . The name must be there; it's just a question of which name.'

'You really believe you can solve this, don't you?' Donald asked in a curiously tentative tone.

'Should bloody hope so, Donald. She's had us haring all over the place this morning; better be worth it,' Veronica piped up.

Daphne turned and looked out of the window, at the fields on either side of them as they hurtled through the Surrey roads back to town. Should bloody hope so indeed.

25

Veronica and Donald wished her luck as she set off from the hotel back towards the Theatre Royale. Why Tyrone had insisted on meeting here there, she couldn't say. Possibly he was going to revel in the theatrics of it all: unveil some great and profound truth replete with spotlights and puffs of smoke.

There was no police officer on the stage door now.

'Apparently, it's no longer urgent,' Nigel explained, shrugging. 'Your mate, Inspector Marklow, he seemed to think he didn't need to be here any more. I popped to the pub – couldn't stand that young constable breathing down my neck. When I came back, they'd all buggered off.'

Daphne gave a shrug in solidarity with Nigel's bafflement. 'Haven't seen Tyrone Bridge, have you, Nigel?'

Donald's dressing room struck Daphne as an odd place for Tyrone to be waiting for her, but, Nigel explained, it was where Mr Bridge was waiting.

The dressing room was at the end of the corridor, neighboured by a costume wardrobe and a miserably small kitchenette, whose only purpose, it seemed, was to house an endless supply of glasses and several broken bottle openers. Donald, of course, felt that he'd drawn the short straw in being allocated this one, and had let his indignation be known on numerous occasions over the preceding days.

'Tyrone, hello? It's Daphne.' She tapped on the door, then trilled a yoohoo. Not a peep. Perhaps he had gone to the bar. Or, more likely, was snooping around trying to scrape up some dirt to print in his noxious column. Emboldened, she now rapped sharply on the door, ear pressed up against it. An indistinct sound came from within. 'Tyrone? I hope you're decent – I'm coming in.'

Opening the door, her first impression was of disorder. A bouquet of roses had been overturned, the stems strewn across the floor. An assortment of lotions and potions, creams and compresses were similarly dispersed across the dressing table, the stool for which had been knocked over.

As Daphne's eye roved over all of this, she felt herself hit by a wave of apprehension which left her feeling cold. She froze when she spotted the shape slumped in the corner. A shape that moved.

Daphne approached cautiously but with determination.

It was, without question, a person. Tyrone Bridge. A leg was twisted unnaturally, pointing towards Daphne. She knelt down quickly, her hands shaking as she reached towards him.

Tyrone Bridge's face stared back at her, his mouth gaping in a terrible O. At his neck was a trickle of blood. More than a trickle. Something was protruding from his neck ... Daphne gasped when she realised what it was: the pen. He had been stabbed with the pen from Chester's parcel, the pen that had been stolen from the safe.

Tyrone's bulging eyes were unblinking, a deathly pallor in his face. Yet he was not dead, not quite. A weak breath fled his mouth. He seemed to recognise Daphne.

'Tyrone, Mr Bridge!' she said loudly. 'Hold on. I'll call for an ambulance.'

With one hand he grasped her arm, his grip surprisingly firm. He was battling to say something, she realised. She leaned as close as she could. He mouthed something, gasped a word. She could barely make it out. She didn't speak, ask him to repeat it, lest she miss anything else. Again a gasp. Then nothing. Stillness.

Daphne looked at Tyrone Bridge, dead on the floor of the dressing room.

She stood up, breathing heavily, attempting to keep herself from succumbing to horror and fear. He had been killed, about that there could be no doubt, and before he had died he had spoken a single word. *Grace*.

She must call for help. Daphne turned to the door. A shadow was approaching. The killer? Back for more? She froze. Her pulse, already thrumming, quickened. She glanced around the room and grabbed an empty champagne bottle. A blow with it could earn her the chance to flee. She wasn't going down without a fight. She was Daphne King, damn it.

The shadow grew. The figure was getting nearer. She tightened her grip on the bottle, steadied herself, slowed her breathing.

She could hear a low muttering as the figure approached. *I'll give you something to mutter about, you murderous wretch*, Daphne thought to herself.

The doorway was filled by the figure.

'Inspector Marklow?' she exclaimed with incredulity. 'How on earth did you get here so quickly? I haven't even—'

'Daphne, where's Hartforth?' The inspector's directness made it clear he had no time to answer any questions.

'Hartforth? You m-mean Donald?' Daphne stammered, replacing the bottle on the side. 'I don't know. I just arrived here to speak with Tyrone, and . . .' She stood aside and gestured towards Tyrone Bridge's dead body.

'Christ alive,' Marklow blurted. 'Another one.'

Before Daphne had the chance to ask yet another question (pertinent in her view, inane in Marklow's), the inspector had summoned PC Lott and told him to stay put. 'Don't let anyone near that body, Lott. Heads'll roll if you do, and by that I mean yours. Daphne, come with me. This place is a rabbit warren, but you seem to know your way about. We need to find Hartforth.'

Confusion rising within her, Daphne contained herself and swiftly overtook Marklow, leading him through the interminable corridors.

Daphne felt beads of sweat form on her brow. Her throat was dry, her skin prickly, a knot had tied itself around her innards. The elation of her discoveries, the thrill she had felt at her schoolgirl detective larks, were gone. This wasn't a lark at all. If she had arrived at the dressing room just a little earlier, she might well have been lying in a heap on the floor too. There was a killer running amok, and Daphne had placed herself directly in their murderous path.

Suddenly, there ahead of them, Donald was approaching, with Irene just behind him.

'What's the commotion, Daphne? Robert's not risen from the dead to visit us all, has he?' Donald asked, lazily brushing his hand through his hair. 'Oh, your policeman friend is here again. Hello, Inspector. What can we—'

Marklow had rushed forward, bundling Donald to the ground in what Daphne perceived to be a somewhat heavy-handed fashion. As Donald struggled, demanding to know what the devil was happening, Marklow informed him of his arrest, and Irene began shrieking, an incessant, repetitive shrieking that Daphne feared would never stop.

'... for the murder of Robert Stirling,' Marklow declared. 'Most likely for that other poor sod back in your dressing room too.'

With that Daphne could contain herself no longer. Doubling over, she vomited onto the carpet.

26

In the weeks, months and indeed years that followed the vomiting was the one detail that Daphne omitted from every retelling of the events of December 1935. The other details she would describe in intricate and vivid terms, each retelling bringing a new and startling revelation. Clues she could have spotted earlier, intonations of voice that unwittingly disclosed truths, questions she wished she had asked.

Marklow roughly pulled Donald to his feet, locking a pair of handcuffs on him.

'I don't understand, Marklow. You think he murdered Robert?' Daphne said incredulously, dabbing the corners of her mouth with her handkerchief. The words were failing to make sense to her even as she spoke them.

'Bloody hell, Miss King,' Marklow said rather breathless, the scuffle having exhausted him. He peered at the off-putting puddle of vomit. 'You alright there?'

Daphne frowned and brushed away his enquiry with a flick of the wrist.

'Of course I didn't murder him!' Donald protested, his face twisted in horror. 'Why would I *murder* him? That's nonsense!'

'Why indeed, eh Hartforth,' Marklow echoed. 'Tried to pull the wool over our eyes, but we're not as stupid as you think.'

Daphne reeled. This all seemed highly improbable.

'Marklow, why ... How do you know it was Donald?'

'I'm not at liberty to disclose that information, Miss King.' Marklow reverted to an officious manner in moments of stress. It was a tic that Daphne had noticed on many previous occasions, but never had it irked her more than now. 'It's an open investigation, and all you need know is that we have strong reason to believe that Mr Hartforth here has blood on his hands. That is why he has been taken into custody.'

'But *why* would Donald kill Robert?' Daphne asked, more to herself than to Marklow.

'Anonymous tip-offs don't tend to go into the whys and wherefores,' Marklow said, his exasperation plain.

So there was the police's evidence: an anonymous tip-off.

None of this fitted with her hypothesis. Donald was

linked to neither the mushrooms, nor the postcards, nor the pen . . . In addition to which, he had been with her all day, so how the devil could he have killed Tyrone? She started, 'Now look here, Marklow, this is preposterous. He's no murderer, he's just a silly actor!'

Marklow ignored her and hauled Donald down the corridor to the stage door and out of the theatre, where, to the combined astonishment of the inspector, Donald and Daphne, they were confronted with a throng of reporters and photographers. Shouts went up: 'Donald!' and 'Is it true?' and 'Why did you want him dead?'

'I'm innocent! Innocent, I tell you! This is a travesty of justice!' Donald cried, flicking his hair out of his eyes. Marklow attempted to manhandle him through the mob towards his police car, but Donald resisted, chanting, 'Justice for Hartforth! Justice for Hartforth!'

The absurdity of the situation could not be denied. Nor could Daphne isolate any single emotion that she was experiencing: she felt appalled, shocked, disbelieving. She was also abominably tired and still felt slightly sick. Robert Stirling had been murdered. Tyrone Bridge had also been murdered. Donald Hartforth had been arrested. And here she was, at the heart of it all.

27

Daphne watched impotently as Donald was bundled into the police car by Marklow and his colleague.

The inspector turned to her. 'Well? You seem rather certain that our Mr Hartforth's not the culprit. Got any bright ideas of your own? Please do enlighten me. As you can see, it is December 23rd, yet I am not at home. Because of this bleedin' case. So anything you can do to send me back to my irate wife would be bloomin' marvellous.'

Daphne hesitated. Marklow had always been forth-coming when she had pumped him for information. And she had always reciprocated. She often overheard remarks by or had been trusted with observations by the kind of people the police tended to overlook: domestic staff and cleaners – people, women usually, who seemed invisible to the police but who absorbed valuable information. It had made for a fruitful professional relationship, Mark-low disclosing the police's stance on a case, Daphne offering proof that they were mistaken. On this particular occasion, however, Daphne found that she did not feel inclined to share her findings.

She didn't want to tell him about the parcels addressed to Chester, the apparent pranks that had nonetheless put him and Theodora on edge. The argument between Robert and George Salter just hours before Robert had been found dead. The photograph of Chester and Robert and Tyrone and Cecil Milford's mother. The retirement home in Little Grinton and its population of poisonous mushrooms.

Nor did she feel disposed to inform Inspector Marklow about Tyrone's dying utterance and the strong sensation she had that this terrible business wasn't over yet. Everything felt ... in the balance. Delicate. To inform Marklow would be to drape a red rag over a bull's eyes and send it directly into a china shop. No, better to keep all she knew under her hat. For now.

'No. Drawing blanks,' Daphne replied. 'But I am absolutely certain that Donald is innocent.'

Irene had followed them out into the street. Her banshee-like wailing had continued, and she now ran towards Marklow and Daphne.

'He's innocent! Donald didn't do anything! It's these people – it's these damned bloody people! They've had it in for him from day one, of course they're pleased as punch to throw wild accusations his way!' She began beating her hands ineffectually against Marklow's chest.

'Come on, Irene, let's get you out of here,' Daphne murmured. 'There's nothing more we can do here.'

Marklow confirmed this. The entire theatre had been declared the scene of a crime, for who knew where Donald – the killer – might have hidden further weapons or stashed evidence that would strengthen the police's case against him. Nobody would be allowed in, and there absolutely wouldn't be any flippin' performance that evening.

The press hounds were still loitering outside the stage door, whipped into a frenzy by the cavalcade of police vehicles that had arrived and departed.

'Shameless vultures, all of them,' Daphne said as she guided a shuffling Irene through the melee. 'Don't say a word to any of them.'

But the press pack was perfectly content without any words from Daphne and Irene. Photographs of the harried pair, elbowing and jostling their way across the road, would be splashed across the next day's newspapers. Readers waking up on Christmas Eve – for tomorrow was Christmas Eve – would recognise Irene as that girl making good in the West End. They would notice her hunched shoulders, her downcast demeanour. Those same readers would also study the woman beside her, the one with spectacles and slightly untamed hair. Some, the most observant among them, would note the determination in this woman's eyes – not the haunted or dazed expression worn by her companion, but the look of a woman with work to do.

28

By the time Daphne reached the Regency Hotel, the group had already gathered in the bar. A telephone call from Nigel had broken the news of Tyrone's murder and Donald's arrest. Although to do so seemed entirely inappropriate, Daphne felt rather amused. As glum and drab as it was, the bar of the Regency Hotel was undoubtedly the most fitting venue in all of London for the tense discussions that the company of *A Christmas Carol* relished. She braced herself for the onslaught that was to come.

Panic, or fear, or sadness . . . whatever hybrid of emotions they were feeling, had amplified each person's characters; they were almost pastiches of themselves. Veronica's insouciance looked forced, affected in this room. Chester sat ashen-faced in the armchair he appeared to have adopted for occasions such as these. Theodora stood behind him, her hands resting upon his shoulder protectively. Their splendour dimmed by the events, the couple seemed far more mundane now: a forty-five-year-old woman struggling to comfort her much older husband. Alfred, perched on a stool, called to mind a nervous sparrow, his leg jiggling uncontrollably. Irene had begun to sob again, while Cecil sat beside her looking withdrawn, his legs crossed. George Salter had joined the group, his beady eyes scanning the room for weakness like a shark sweeping for blood.

Veronica approached Daphne and squeezed her arms, 'Hell's bells, Daphne, are you all right? Nigel said it was you who . . . who found Tyrone.'

Daphne nodded. 'Yes, that's right. Becoming an unfortunate habit of mine.'

'I'll bet your editor thinks quite the contrary – got himself an inside scoop on a double murder,' Veronica said with a wink.

There followed a debate between company members as to what to do next. Theodora argued that they should all go their separate ways, back to their rooms. For what good could come of wallowing in the gloom of *the happenings*, as they had euphemistically come to be known. Veronica contested this, claiming that they ought to thrash it out together – get to the bottom of this 'mucky business'. She had almost said 'deliciously mucky' but had bitten her tongue.

Chester had the final say.

'One member of our company is dead. Another has been arrested. Tyrone Bridge was found murdered in *our* theatre. I for one would like to know what is happening, and hiding in my hotel room will not help with that,' he said. The weariness in his voice was to be expected. There was a sadness to it, however, that affected them all. This was no melodrama, no cheap potboiler, no fanciful story.

The decision made – that they should sit and thrash it out – there remained the question of what to drink. Here, the debate took a surreal turn, Daphne once more having the curious sensation of watching herself from afar. A man had been murdered – no, *two* men had been murdered – yet here they were, heatedly discussing how many bottles of Languedoc to order. It has been noted that in times of crisis the human spirit clings to the most prosaic of practicalities, wrestling disorder into something resembling order. At last, after what seemed like an age, the wine was ordered from the barman, who seemed distinctly put out by the prospect of having to do his job.

Glasses of red wine distributed, they sat uneasily, nobody entirely certain about how to proceed. Daphne's eyes flitted around the loose circle, loath to settle on anybody in particular.

'Well, here's to Robert,' Theodora uttered. 'An actor till the end.'

'And to Tyrone,' Chester added. 'A lover of high drama till the end.'

Raising their glasses and taking hearty gulps of wine, the group seemed to take a collective sigh of relief.

'I'm sorry, this is beyond the pale. Remind me why I'm here with you all?' Irene, her voice hoarse from wailing, spoke first. 'Not one of you lifted a finger to help Donald, and *you* –' here she threw an accusing finger towards Daphne '– led the coppers straight to him.'

This was Daphne's prompt to clarify and elaborate on all the preceding events. Tyrone's death – murder. Robert Stirling's death – murder. Marklow's explanation for his arrest of Donald. She delivered her account in a sober and detached tone. Sparing herself and her listeners the more gruesome aspects of the scene in Donald's dressing room, she skipped over certain details. Nobody need hear about the grotesque sight of Tyrone Bridge's eyes swivelling in terror. It was for a different reason entirely, however, that she decided to keep another detail under her hat – that of Tyrone gasping the name Grace at the last.

Chester shook his head, groping for words but finding none.

'It doesn't make any sense – none of this adds up. It's barmy,' Alfred said.

'It's more than barmy, Alfred. Let's not mince our words: it's completely mad is what it is,' his sister rejoined.

Alfred continued, 'Why would Donald murder Robert? And Tyrone?'

Daphne was emphatic. 'He didn't. I've an inkling about what happened – why Donald's been arrested, I mean. I need to . . . ascertain a few things first, but I will stake my life on the fact that Donald had absolutely nothing to do with either murder.'

Theodora's voice was heavy with exhaustion. 'Perhaps he did though. Perhaps it was jealousy of Robert? Anger at Tyrone? Petty motivations, but then Donald is a petty creature. And not, we can all agree, the brightest.'

'He's a dunce,' George Salter sneered. 'Seen guys kill for less. He wants his name up in bright lights – gets ridda Robert. That Bridge guy – sticks and stones and all that, but seems to me that Donald had enough of being called names. Gets ridda him too. Plain sailing.'

'Except it's not, is it, Mr Salter?' Veronica pointed out. 'He's been arrested. Not likely to be many starring roles in Wormwood Scrubs. Bloody silly thing to do.'

'Which is why it seems perfectly reasonable to me

that he *did* do it. A silly thing to do, and Donald Hartforth *is* silly,' Theodora argued.

Daphne was struck by Theodora's vehemence. She was running a string of pearls through her fingers, her customary *froideur* less pronounced than usual. While Daphne contemplated Theodora's agitation, the curtains covering the door to the bar parted to reveal Lilian Rogers. Dressed in an outfit identical to the one she had been wearing yesterday, Lilian evidently saw no need for pleasantries, but strode directly over.

'Well, this is a fine mess you've got my client into,' she said, removing her black gloves. 'The press are going to love this.' A look, not quite contemptuous but not far off it, was thrown in Daphne's direction.

'Daphne's not here because of that,' Veronica said defensively. 'She's the one who found Tyrone in Donald's dressing room. She'll probably be carted off by the police soon to give a statement, or whatever it is one does when one finds a nearly dead body.'

'Nearly dead?' Lilian asked.

'Nearly dead when I found him,' Daphne confirmed, taking a sip of her wine. 'Dead shortly thereafter. Still dead now. One hopes – assumes, I mean. One assumes.' Another sip of wine to steady herself.

'Fact of the matter is, the police seem pretty damned certain that Donald killed Robert. Who knows what the man's capable of?' Chester said, words suddenly spilling out of him.

Daphne frowned. The assumption of Donald's guilt was being made far too readily by certain among the group, she thought. 'Why is it that suddenly you're very eager to pin the blame on Donald?' she blurted before she could stop herself.

Nobody answered, but in the silence that followed she could feel the unease rising.

'If it wasn't Donald, that would mean someone else did it. Do you have any thoughts on that front, Daphne?' Cecil's voice had no malice, no irony. In fact, the question was posed with no discernible feeling at all. He looked at Daphne with a smile that, though artless, or because of its artlessness, was entirely disarming.

'Don't be absurd, Cecil,' Theodora snapped unexpectedly. 'She's stirring the pot, that's what journalists do.'

'Theodora, I think it a perfectly reasonable line of enquiry. Daphne is merely asking a question which, if we're civilised, rational beings, we ought all to be asking. After all, we do live in a world where one is innocent until proven guilty,' Lilian interjected. 'Where guilt has been proven, let punishment fall.'

'Quite.' Daphne felt vindicated if a little surprised by Lilian's defence of her. 'And if Donald's innocent, the police will soon realise that, and he'll have nothing to fear.'

'Oh now on that point I must disagree,' Lilian countered. 'The innocent have perhaps more to fear in this world than most others. However, in this matter we must hope the police will root out the truth. Your friend Inspector Marklow can be relied upon?'

Before Daphne could answer, Cecil chimed in, 'Nothing for it now but to wait.'

'Wait? Wait for what? Wait for Donald to be locked up and the key thrown away? Damned if I'm sitting around here with all of *you*,' Irene shouted, tears streaming down her face. Abruptly, she stood up, barging her way out of the bar. 'There's something going on here, you all know it!'

Daphne glanced at Veronica. Was that an imperceptible nod of the head, a slight widening of the eyes and raising of the eyebrows? Daphne thought so, and, making her excuses, she left the bar too – followed by Veronica.

29

'Right. Put your coat on. We're getting out of this infernal hotel and you're to tell me everything that's happened since we returned from Little Grinton, understand?' Veronica barked her instructions with all the vigour of a games mistress telling her gals to hop to it.

Outside, a gaggle of Christmas carollers roved along the street, their smiling faces intended to spread tidings of comfort and joy but instead underlining the gaping lack thereof in Daphne's afternoon. Or evening? She glanced at her wristwatch: only four o'clock. It felt like days since she had skipped through Little Grinton, buoyed up by pride in her own ingenuity.

'I think I ought to wrap my head around everything before I . . . before I share it with anyone.' Daphne affected an unconvincingly breezy manner.

Veronica was leaning against the wall outside the hotel, one hand in her trouser pocket, the other raised, holding a cigarette. It was, Daphne suspected, a pose that Veronica had perfected over many years of loitering. A pose intended to intimidate and fluster, aggravate and intoxicate. 'Oh how fascinating,' she replied. 'Pity that you're entirely overruled. I shall brook no counterarguments.'

Daphne flushed with . . . embarrassment? Irritation? Two murders appeared to have taken place right under her nose, and she – crusading beacon of journalistic perspicacity – was still scrambling to piece it all together. She knew that it was there, it was within reach, but every time she clutched at it, the truth slipped away.

'Actually, Veronica,' she babbled in an unbecomingly shrill voice, 'it's none of your concern what happened. I'm under no obligation to pour out my heart to you, though you may be used to that. But I can tell you, I'm made of sterner stuff. You can't just . . . pout at me and wave your cigarette and magically I'll reveal all of my innermost thoughts and tell you what I f— What are you doing? Where are we going?'

Veronica had sidled over, looped her arm through Daphne's and was beginning to lead her away from the hotel. 'We're going to the pub, and you're going to tell me all of your innermost thoughts and precisely what it is you found.'

Reluctantly allowing herself to be led by Veronica through the crowds of Soho – four o'clock was evidently the hour at which the denizens of the neighbourhood saw fit to rise and go about their business – Daphne felt a sense of resignation mixed with relief. She was, she feared, beginning to lose sight of the wood for her fixation on the trees. Perhaps taking Veronica into her confidence would unscramble her mind, allow some of the pieces of the puzzle to be fitted into an intelligible pattern.

The pub that Veronica escorted her into was a cosy affair, but a table in a corner gave them a degree of privacy. The panelling of the walls was a deep mahogany, interspersed with dulled mirroring. The only concession to Christmas was a rather miserable-looking miniature conifer, which drooped in the pot it sat in atop the bar.

Another pub, another gin, Daphne reflected.

'Sausage roll *and* peanuts.' Veronica placed the food on the table, flicking away some crumbs as she did. 'Never let it be said that Veronica Burford doesn't know how to treat her ladies.'

'I'll thank you to omit the possessive pronoun, Miss Burford,' Daphne said as she grabbed a handful of peanuts with very little in the way of inhibition.

'Now, are you going to tell me what you've sniffed out, or do I have to winkle it out of you?' Veronica asked.

Daphne sighed. A deep sigh. And then she told Veronica everything. All the peculiar happenstances that as yet floated untethered in a stagnant pool of doubt and suspicion. The unanswered questions were too numerous to count. Why had Robert and George Salter been arguing about money? Who had sent the cryptic notes and objects to Chester? Not to mention Little Grinton and that blasted photograph of Chester, Robert, Tyrone and Cecil's mother. And then there were the mushrooms and the pen. Two very particular choices of murder weapon.

Then it struck her: the visitors' book from the old folks' home – she hadn't checked the page she had torn out thoroughly yet. She pulled it from her satchel and unfolded it in front of the bowl of peanuts.

'Anything familiar? Anything at all?' she asked Veronica.

Frowning, Veronica shook her head. 'Nope. None of these names mean anything, I'm afraid, Daphne.'

There had to be something. Hurling another handful of peanuts into her mouth, Daphne persevered. The page had columns for the date and time of each visitor's arrival, the name of the visitor and the name of the resident they had come to see.

Mrs Plumber had visited a *Bob P*; there was an *Isobel* who had visited *Russell R*, then *Edward Smythe* to see *Nancy D*.

But there was nothing. Daphne felt deflated. After her

instincts had been proved right about the postcards, she had expected the universe to drop the answers into her lap.

Some cheering erupted across the pub. A party had arrived, and a woman was producing coloured paper crowns from a bag.

'Let's assess what we have,' Veronica began, then, prompted by Daphne's raised eyebrow, 'what *you* have, I mean.'

The postcards first. Daphne laid them out on the table, devouring the last of the sausage roll to make space.

'Now, as we've already established, the postcards correspond with the stops on the tour. Scarborough, Margate, etcetera, etcetera. It's the messages we need to examine more closely now. They're riddles, really.'

Printed neatly, uniformly, no leaning loops or unsteady letters. She pored over the messages. Unclear in their meaning, they were nevertheless vaguely threatening in tone.

Blackpool – Worms may turn, but time will not.
Margate – Women who rage are thrown in
*   asylums; men who rage are given the keys.*
Scarborough – An honest saint is more
*   dangerous than a lying sinner.*

'*Grace,*' Veronica said. For the first time that afternoon – possibly since Daphne had first met her – she appeared less than composed.

Daphne was rather pleased that Veronica seemed at last to have been stumped by something. 'Come again?'

'These . . . Well, I might be mistaken,' Veronica said, 'but I think these are quotes from *Grace.*'

'Grace who?' was Daphne's immediate question.

'*A Woman of Grace and Fury* – Chester's play.'

The play. The play that Chester had written and directed over twenty years ago. The play that, after years of wandering in a wilderness of theatrical mediocrity and critical indifference, had catapulted him to overnight success. The only play he had ever written.

'That was Tyrone's final word!' Daphne exclaimed, spilling her drink and almost toppling the table. '*Grace*! I thought he wanted me to give a message to someone – a loved one, his mother, I don't know. But he was saying *Grace* – the play!'

Veronica frowned. 'So it's the *play* that's the link. The *play* is pointing us towards something.'

'No, it isn't.' Daphne took off her glasses. 'The play isn't doing anything. It's the *killer* that's pointing us towards the play, Veronica. The person who *killed* Robert and Tyrone, the person who sent the postcards to Chester. They're messages.'

The sands were shifting, the tea leaves were settling. Daphne rotated her gin glass, gazing into it as though the answer – or answers – nestled among the fast-melting ice cubes at the bottom. She was hesitant about leaping to any conclusions, weaving strands together with a thread that might snap if it were pulled with any force. The postcards and Tyrone's gasp, the play that Chester had written. Her mind went back to the photograph – it must hold further clues.

There they stood, the four figures, a bustling bar behind them. Smiling, the West End before them. Chester was yet to write *A Woman of Grace and Fury*, Tyrone yet to become a name to strike fear and excitement into the hearts of his targets, mirth and exasperation into his readers. The Phoenix, that had been the name of the pub that Tyrone had mentioned just last night, the pub that had witnessed the escapades of Chester and Robert.

She pulled the photograph from her satchel and laid it beside the postcards.

'Ah yes, angelic Cecil's mother,' Veronica said, peering at it. 'Just the looker I'd imagine producing such a gorgeous son.'

Daphne frowned. 'Save your ogling for another day, Veronica; we're looking for clues.'

Scrunching up her nose in concentration, Daphne scanned the photograph painstakingly. The foreground, she knew intimately by now; Daphne could reel off any number of facts about the people who stood in front of the bar. Chester's left shoelace was undone; Josie Milford had two clips on the left side of her head, one on the right; Robert had, Daphne suspected, a touch of spinach stuck between his front teeth; Tyrone's bow tie was ever so slightly skewed to the left. The background, however, Daphne had ignored, so fixated had she been on this quartet.

Peering beyond them now, she scanned the bar top. Looking for what, she wasn't entirely sure. A message scrawled in lipstick telling her who the killer was? No, Daphne thought, it wouldn't be that easy – nor, she reflected, did she want it to be. The spirit bottles on the shelves behind the group were unremarkable, no encoded labels or messages hidden in hieroglyphics. A few empty pint glasses perched on the end of the bar. An ashtray smouldered, next to it a cigar box.

'Imperial cigars,' Daphne murmured. Someone had mentioned *Imperial* cigars before. 'Chester . . . Chester said that the cigars he had been sent by the . . . prankster were Imperial.'

She was getting warmer, she knew it. Despair was giving way to excitement. Closer, closer. Hanging above the bar was the crest of the pub: a phoenix, blazing majestically, fearsomely above the barman.

Something in Daphne's mind clicked.

Later, Veronica would tell her that at that moment Daphne's face drained of all colour, that she emitted an indecipherable noise, that the ardour in her eyes was most becoming.

She picked up the photograph, held it closer. Squinted. *Was that it, there?* She groaned. *Too small.* She rummaged in her satchel once more. It was, Daphne decided, the moment to show Veronica quite how serious a sleuth she was.

'Daphne, is that a . . . magnifying glass?' Veronica asked incredulously, her eyes twinkling with amusement.

'Naturally,' Daphne confirmed casually. She rarely had recourse to this item, but she was glad that the opportunity had arisen. The glass, with its mother-of-pearl handle and brass trimmings, had cost her a pretty penny, and she was rather taken with how debonair she felt when wielding it.

'Veronica, I want you to look closely, look very closely indeed at the barman!' Daphne was blazing with excitement. 'Tell me what you see . . . in his shirt pocket.' She passed Veronica the magnifying glass.

Veronica peered, murmured something then exclaimed, 'Bust my buttons, Daphne, it's the pen! That bloody pen! It's in the barman's pocket!' She gazed at Daphne in awe. 'You were right – it's all connected! You brilliant creature.'

'It means that the photograph, the pen . . . they *are* the keys to it. Well, that along with the poisoned mushrooms, of course. I knew it! Mother always told me to listen to my waters. I thought she was being daft, but it's true. My waters told me!' Realising what she had just said, Daphne was overcome once more by embarrassment.

'My, my, Daphne. Mothers, waters . . . solving crime really is an intense business, isn't it.'

The brief return to repartee made them both smile. Daphne, invigorated by the discovery of the pen, returned to the photograph. *There must be something else here, something that will shed further light.*

Veronica's face hovered somewhere between incredulity and awe. 'That's the cigars and the pen, but the other little present was a bottle of nondescript plonk. Don't tell me you can find an identical bottle in the photograph too?'

'We don't need to; the cigars and the pen are enough, Veronica. The gifts were sent by someone who wanted Chester to remember this pub – someone who knew the pub too. They were warnings – threats. They gave Chester the willies – reminders of a pub he spent time in twenty years ago. The question is: what did they want him to remember?' Daphne was lost in thought, her words emerging unbidden. 'Tyrone and Robert are dead. They must have known what happened there, they *must* have done. If they knew the secret, killing them would keep them silent . . .'

'Daphne, don't you think you're getting a little . . . overexcited? Making too many assumptions?'

Daphne glared at her. 'Veronica, please. I'm in no mood for being belittled or patronised. If I want that, the bus to the *Chronicle*'s office stops just around the corner. What I need from you is focus.'

Veronica appeared chastened, even a little irritated by this response. A moment passed, during which Daphne reflected that even the most determined investigator needed an obliging assistant on hand. She couldn't afford to have hers out of sorts.

She turned to Veronica and sighed, 'Well, now that we have that little spat out of the way, how do you fancy accompanying me on a little errand?'

30

This particular errand required Veronica to follow Daphne as she sped towards a London institution that, she revealed, had provided her with years of succour and hours of relief: Foyles. She had relied on the bookshop for much. The red lettering above its doors signalled a haven amid the hectic pedestrian traffic along Charing Cross Road. The stacks of books within welcomed and lulled her. Here, she could find thrills and insights that would transport her from her room in Camberwell. Having read about Nellie Bly's journalistic exploits, Daphne had badgered the beleaguered booksellers every week, hunting out any titles with even a passing reference to Bly and her investigations.

As they entered, a studious-looking woman quietly informed them that the shop would be closing in one hour.

'Never fear, we know precisely what we're here for.' Daphne smiled at the woman.

Lingering just a moment beside the popular fiction

section (Daphne made mental notes as to which titles she would return for at a later, less urgent date), Daphne steered Veronica upstairs.

'Now, I've heard tell of your sort: women who lure their prey to dubious bookshops, dragging them down into a moral turpitude from which escape is impossible,' Veronica said jovially.

'Moral turpitude is quite right, Veronica, an absolute quagmire of it. Though this ought to be one with which you're already very familiar,' Daphne replied, gesturing towards the sign at the end of an aisle that announced that they had reached the drama section.

The penny dropped. Veronica laughed. 'If Madame will allow me to escort her past dear old Euripedes – no time for any of his Dionysian bacchanals. Keep going, if you please, don't stop at John Ford. Ah, here we are: H for Harrison. *A Woman of Grace and Fury.*'

Both women armed with a copy of the book that Daphne knew they must scour, they sat down on the floor in front of the shelves.

'Are you going to tell me what it is we're looking for, Daphne?' her companion asked after realising that nothing would be gained by demonstrative sighs or repeated declarations that a bottle of wine would make their task a damn sight easier.

Daphne glanced up from the book and chewed her

bottom lip. 'Well, there's the rub . . . I can't quite define what it is we're on the hunt for. All I know is that I'll be certain when I've found it. Anything odd, anything that strikes you as . . . noteworthy,' she replied.

'Noteworthy, right-o. Thank you, Miss King, for your targeted and specific directions. Perhaps to be even more focused and rigorous we ought to read some tea leaves, maybe take a look at some Tarot cards,' Veronica burbled, flicking through the pages haphazardly. 'You know I've read this several times already? Chester was a hero to me after he wrote it. I was only a youngster, thirteen, fourteen, but it made quite the impression. Point is, I'm not exactly a pair of unbiased eyes.'

Daphne grinned. 'Which is precisely why your presence here is required. Given your years spent poring over Chester's words, I'll be grateful for your interpretation of any lines I stumble upon that seem . . .'

'Noteworthy,' Veronica finished.

'Right. And while we're on the topic of writing . . . When's Chester going to read your play, give you those nuggets of industry wisdom you've been seeking?' Daphne asked casually, glancing at the photograph of Chester on the inside flyleaf of the book. Dressed in a black jumper, with a cravat about his neck, Chester's chin rested upon his fist, his signet ring catching the light.

'Hmm. The conclusion I've come to is that Chester

would rather not dip his toes in the waters of modern European theatre,' Veronica replied.

A handful of customers trailed past their makeshift reading station, reminding Daphne that they were pressed for time.

'No, reading this, I can't say that Chester's style is an obvious fit with your particular genre of . . . hair-rending and teeth-gnashing,' Daphne commented. 'Lots of moralising and pontificating, if you ask me. I thought Chester in his youth was a bit of a hell-raiser, not a preacher: "Where guilt has been proven, let punishment fall."'

'I'm fairly confident that the scenes in French are quite saucy. One can get away with anything if one is speaking French, *n'est ce pas*?' Veronica's Gallic accent was almost as convincing as Donald's Scottish effort earlier in Little Grinton.

'Come again?' Daphne's eyes darted towards Veronica.

'*N'est ce pas*. It means—'

'I'm perfectly aware of what it means, Veronica. But French scenes? Where are the French scenes?' Daphne flicked through the pages, until Veronica pointed her towards Act 3 Scene 4.

Isobel: *Est-ce que ça peut être toi? Mon cher frère?*
Rostand: *Ma sœur! Bien que nous ayons été séparés, nous nous élèverons ensemble, forts.*

A whirring began in Daphne's mind. Siblings, grief, strength – this was what the play explored. Ideas were rearranging themselves in her mind, slipping into place.

'Veronica, we need search no longer,' she exclaimed. 'We need to make two more stops: the police station and the Phoenix pub. Not necessarily in that order. *Allons-y!*'

31

Over the preceding twenty-four hours, Daphne had gained a faith in her abilities and a confidence in her instincts that she had never experienced before. Away from the stifling offices of the *Chronicle*, without Martin Halliday greeting every suggestion she made with a condescending smile, Daphne felt liberated. This mad scheme was, she was certain, going to work. Everything Veronica had told her, everything she herself had gleaned and stored away, everything she had read. It all pointed towards one conclusion.

The Phoenix pub lay just south of Charing Cross Road, and, time being of the essence in Daphne's words, they had taken the bus. The ride there allowed Daphne and Veronica a glimpse of the shop fronts and pubs with their baubles and tinsel. Daphne realised that, for the first time this season, she was feeling some Christmas cheer. Oddly, the unravelling of a mystery, the chasing down of a killer, seemed to inspire in Daphne King some festive warmth.

Jumping off the bus, Daphne reminded Veronica of the plan – not just for their stint in the pub, but for later that evening too. The plan that involved calling Alfred at the Regency and initiating the final steps that needed to be taken.

'Daphne, this all sounds a little . . . hare-brained to me,' Veronica had muttered when Daphne shared her newly formulated strategy. 'But you're in luck; hare-brained is precisely how I like my schemes. And I know my brother – he'll be all too happy to oblige. He'll get them all to the theatre, my dear.'

Inside the pub, the Christmas spirit was very much in evidence. A piano in the corner was surrounded by rev-ellers swinging their pints above their heads to the tune and joining in with the pianist's bellowing of 'Oh what fun it is to ride in a one-horse open sleigh!' Daphne reflected that she would be happier when not assailed by carols with such regularity.

The saloon, which boasted a high ceiling and an elab-orate chandelier, seemed to rock to and fro under the weight of the exuberance held within it. Not a corner of the room could be seen without a string of tinsel or a silver trumpet-playing cherub hanging from it, and

Daphne and Veronica had to jostle their way through the merrymakers to reach the bar.

Behind it, barmen and -women flitted hither and thither, calls of 'What can I get yer?' and 'Lemon with that?' making any attempt to chat at the counter futile. Daphne scanned the faces of the staff: *Too young, far too young, too young again . . . Aha!* At around sixty or so, his thin red hair receding, and a well-kept moustache sitting nimbly atop his lip, this fellow was the correct age. Daphne closed her eyes and made a silent supplication to the goddess Themis. Please let this man have worked in the pub in 1912.

Eventually Daphne got his attention, and he approached, cocking his ear towards her.

'Excuse me, might I trouble you to—' Daphne began, shouting over the noise.

Veronica cut in, snatched the photograph from Daphne, and held it up to the man. 'Know him?'

'Him? Course I do!' the man exclaimed, no lengthy examination of the photograph necessary.

'Quick word?' Veronica shouted, shoving a few bob into the man's hand. He nodded to the right, indicating a door to Daphne and Veronica, who pushed their way through the drinkers and went through.

Following them into the storeroom, the barman brought with him a bottle of wine and three glasses.

'Now, ladies, unless I'm mistaken, you're looking for some rather juicy information,' he said. 'I'm Gary, by the way. Pleased to meet you.'

Nodding at them both, for nodding appeared to be Gary's primary mode of communication, he filled the glasses with dark crimson wine. A loud crash and a subsequent cheer were heard through the door.

'Be needing to go and clean that up – whatever the bloody hell it is – so if you'd be so good as to tell me what you're after, I'll do my best and then get on,' Gary said, an unseemly leer appearing on his face.

'We're interested in anything you can tell us about this man,' Daphne said, deliberately maintaining a neutral expression. She had, she fancied, encountered men like Gary before. To react was to encourage. Such was the way of the world. She sighed inwardly.

'Oh yes. Remember him well. Spent the best part of four years here, I reckon. Always spouting poetic mumbo-jumbo. Always scribbling away. Clever bloke, he was. Bloody sight cleverer than that lot who hung about him. Whatever 'appened to 'im?'

Daphne and Veronica exchanged glances.

'Well, Gary, that's a very interesting question,' Daphne replied.

32

Daphne requested silence from Veronica when they once more found themselves on a bus. Side by side, the women sat contemplating the events of the preceding twenty-four hours. Veronica marvelled at the position in which she now found herself: a slapdash Watson of sorts to a mind that moved with unfathomable agility and precision. The machinations of Daphne's brain simply defied Veronica's comprehension. She had always rather fancied herself the cleverest girl in the room, and in many rooms she still would be. But in any room where Daphne King was present, well, Veronica knew she would be playing second fiddle. Some of the events she understood – she had been able to grasp the network which connected the mushrooms, the post-cards, the old folks' home. Other truths that had been unveiled to her, she could not, for all her attempts, make out how Daphne had forged the links. Daphne had explained to her the significance of the shouting that

Irene had overheard – the argument between Robert and George Salter – but still she couldn't see it. How had Daphne worked it out? Veronica glanced up at her, frowning and biting her lip again.

Daphne's mind was whirring. There were a certain number of risks she had taken that day, but all had been calculated. Soon, very soon, she would take the greatest risk yet – confronting the killer – but before that she had a damsel in distress to rescue.

'Here we are!' she said cheerily, as the bus slowed to a stop outside the Police Station of Central West End. As if in rebellion against its alluringly glamorous name, the station – monolithic, grey, achingly characterless – bore down oppressively on any who passed by.

'Oh goodie,' Veronica drawled. 'Can't wait to be reunited with our darling boy.'

Asking for Inspector Marklow at reception, Daphne rocked back and forth on the balls of her feet.

'Feeling sprightly?' Veronica asked, slouching beside her. 'Smug that all your plans are shaping up rather nicely?'

'Oh quite nicely indeed, thank you, Veronica.'

A clock behind the reception desk told Daphne that it was nearing six thirty. By golly but time flew when one was having fun.

'Ah, here you are, Inspector,' Daphne said as

Marklow marched disconsolately towards her. 'And how is your interrogation of Mr Hartforth?'

Marklow sighed at Daphne. 'You know full well how it's going – abysmally. The man's a snivelling wreck. Just keeps repeating that it wasn't him, that he was –' Marklow flicked through his pocketbook '– "just having a bit of fun".' Well, I know what these theatre types classify as "fun" – seen enough of these things get out of hand. We'll get him, though.'

Daphne cleared her throat. 'Marklow, hate to break it to you, but it wasn't Donald.'

'So you keep saying, King. But there's nothing to get him off the hook – he has no alibi for either murder, aside from that young Juniper woman.'

'Allow me to speculate about the anonymous tip-off,' Daphne interjected. 'What are the chances that there wasn't just one but there were two telephone calls made to the station?'

Marklow stood silently, a frown clouding his face.

'I'll wager that one of those telephone calls, the first, was received at . . . oooh, let's say eleven o'clock yesterday morning? From a telephone box in an area just outside London – in, gosh, I'll hazard a guess . . . Surrey? And might I be so bold as to hypothesise that the second was made at around half past three – from a telephone number which, I'm willing to gamble rather a lot on, belongs to the Regency Hotel?' Daphne appeared far too pleased with herself to need external congratulation in the form of Marklow confirming her hypotheses.

'How the bloody hell did you know that?' Marklow demanded.

'Because, Inspector, Donald Hartforth made the calls himself, preening nincompoop that he is,' Daphne explained. 'He was with me all morning, listening to me, another preening nincompoop, boast about my supreme confidence in being able to track down the real killer.'

Veronica furnished Marklow with the remaining pieces of the puzzle. 'Donald would do anything to be in the spotlight. You heard his pre-prepared chant yesterday – "Justice for Hartforth!" Man's a fool for fame. And being wrongly accused of murder and then released after clever old Daphne unmasks the real killer would get dear silly old Donald on the front page of every newspaper.'

Daphne explained that she'd known this, in essence, after approximately ten minutes' cogitating on Donald's arrest and the circumstances surrounding it. This of course displeased Marklow greatly. Did she have any idea how much police time and resources had been wasted on that fool? How apoplectic Nessa was that he had, for a second consecutive evening, failed to return home in time for tea?

'Yes,' Daphne conceded, scratching her head. 'Sorry about that. Thought you might be cross. Which is why I bring you good news: I know who the killer is. Give me one hour, and I'll deliver them directly to you. Now, could we have dear Mr Hartforth back? Please?'

33

As instructed by Daphne, Veronica had called ahead to the Regency Hotel to speak to Alfred. Instructed in turn, he had then gathered the others, knocking on their room doors or locating them in the bar. Certain among the company had been reluctant – Irene for one could see no earthly reason why she should spend any more time with the pack of them. However, Alfred's engaging affability made him the perfect envoy for the task, and they were all duly coaxed into making their way to the Theatre Royale one last time. The police had vacated the premises now, searches conducted, evidence gathered.

An empty theatre is like a haunted house, a ghostly galleon. Dotted around the abandoned stage, the company waited like lost souls in purgatory. Fittingly, the gravestones had not yet been dismantled and removed and loomed like a silent audience to the performances that were to come. Performances of innocence, performances of surprise, performances of reproach.

Cecil was perched on one, his folded arms the only sign of impatience. When Alfred had sought them all out, Theodora had been having a sherry in the hotel bar with Lilian Rogers; the pair now stood uncomfortably, Lilian idly picking at her black gloves, Theodora's unhappiness growing with every passing moment. George Salter, sour and unmoving as ever, had stationed himself stage left. Chester greeted Daphne and Veronica cordially.

'I say, we're all somewhat in the dark here. What have you two cooked up?' he asked.

Veronica and Daphne exchanged glances. 'We wanted everyone to be here for the news,' Daphne began.

As calculated, this opening gambit was enigmatic enough to capture everyone's attention.

'I spoke to the police earlier – with Inspector Marklow,' she continued, glancing around at the faces of her audience. How did guilt betray itself? Who was blinking a trifle too quickly? Her suspicions were only that at the moment. The blank faces before her showed no indication that her theories were correct. 'And he told us the news – the good news. Wonderfully relieving news in some ways.'

'Darling, I hate to say it, but you're milking this,' Theodora said. 'Please do spit it out.'

'It wasn't Donald,' Daphne said, maintaining a level gaze, a cool demeanour. It was all to play for. 'Robert's death, Tyrone's death ... well, their murders. Donald didn't have anything to do with them.'

Irene, who had been sitting at the front of the stage, her legs dangling over the edge, jumped up triumphantly. 'I told you, I *told* you! He'll never forgive you all when he hears how easily you swallowed the police's story. What a load of nonsense. When will he be released?'

'Well, there's the rub,' Veronica chipped in. 'He's not been arrested for murder – hooray, etcetera, etcetera – but he's in a spot of trouble for wasting police time. Marklow rather dug his heels in. Wouldn't let Donald out just yet – wanted him to stew a touch longer.'

Lilian Rogers snorted at this. 'What on *earth* has the dear boy done? He's made a complete fool of himself.'

'Yes, as it happens. Donald ... well, he framed himself. He, er, he decided that being wrongfully arrested for murder might be a publicity coup. "Justice for Hartforth" and all that. Told Marklow he was convinced it would make some waves. Made an anonymous phone call to the police, telling them it was him. But hadn't really thought it through, apparently. Panic set in when he realised he was in quite a lot of hot water – you know, for murdering two people. All quite silly really,' Daphne explained to gasps of incredulity.

'This is utterly preposterous,' Chester spluttered. 'What on earth was he thinking, assing around like that?'

'He was furthering his career prospects, according to him,' Veronica said.

'Damned idiotic way to do it,' Lilian said, contempt oozing from her voice.

To the exasperation of all assembled, Irene was crying again. 'Don't talk about him like that, Lilian! It's all *your* fault we're in this mess in the first place – you're the one who told us to do this play. Neither of us wanted to! All that talk about learning valuable lessons from an old hand – absolute tripe! It's been a shambles from start to finish. If they send Donald to the gallows for this, his blood is on *your* hands.' Irene was pointing at Lilian, her face red with emotion.

'Darling, if you've quite finished,' Lilian said evenly, 'I think it's crucial you understand that they don't hang people for being imbeciles. From that fate at least, Donald will be safe.'

Theodora had been silent, her eyes fixed on Daphne since her arrival. 'You said it was good news, "in some ways". Care to elaborate on this?'

Daphne had been engaged in an intense scrutiny of the faces of her audience – one face in particular – and it took her a moment to answer. 'Yes, well, Donald didn't kill Robert and Tyrone, so someone else did – and they're . . . at large, as they say. Marklow suspects it was someone who had a grudge against them. He's following up on some information as we speak.'

Theodora was glowering now. 'Oh bravo! The inspector is a sorcerer. What powers of divination he possesses! We await with bated breath his next insights.'

The mood in the theatre grew even darker. Nobody seemed to know where to look, certainly not at each other.

'You've no thoughts on the matter, Chester?' Daphne had attempted to pose her question nonchalantly, a passing enquiry that had casually popped into her mind. It had not, however, emerged quite so convincingly.

Chester did little to disguise his surprise. Startled, he immediately looked to Theodora, who returned his glance unblinkingly.

'Thoughts? Come again? What sort of thoughts?' Chester blustered. 'Look, I don't know what you're suggesting, Miss King, but I think we've all had quite enough. We've heard your news, and I think it best we all return to the Regency. The sooner we can leave London and go home, the better.'

Daphne took a deep breath. Here was the moment.

'Quite. Although I should be very careful if I were you, Chester,' she said. 'The killer isn't quite finished yet. As well you know.'

Irene's blubbering came to an abrupt stop. Cecil's imperturbable face cracked slightly, shock seeping into his expression. Even Alfred's leg was stilled. Chester indignantly asked Daphne what the devil she thought she was doing, throwing accusations around.

'What is it that you're suggesting, Daphne?' Cecil asked calmly, approaching Chester and laying a reassuring hand upon his arm.

'I'm suggesting, Cecil, that Chester knows far more about what's been happening than he has said. That he's *always* known far more about it. He hasn't killed anyone, but he is certainly at least partially responsible for their deaths,' Daphne replied equally calmly.

Chester fell silent, his eyes darting wildly from Daphne to his wife. Theodora brought her hand to her face, covering her eyes in a gesture of exhaustion.

'Game's up, Chester,' she said, eyes still obscured. 'Looks like our Miss King has sniffed you out. I *did* tell you it was damnably silly to let her hang around for so long.'

Alfred now was overcome with confusion. 'Hang on a mo. Can someone please explain what's going on here?'

'Yes, perhaps we could cease all this pussy-footing around.' Lilian stood with her hands behind her back. 'Chester, can you enlighten us?'

Daphne watched Chester. He seemed to be revolving

his options in his mind. She waited. They all waited. It was Theodora who broke the silence.

'Let us be clear. Chester had nothing to do with the murders. *Nothing*. He's been in fear of his life since Robert's death. He's been in fear generally for months. Since those gifts started arriving – and those postcards.' Theodora spoke with a protective ardour. She looked at her husband. Chester's shoulders had dropped. The shadows and crevices of his face were no longer distinguished, but haunted and hollow.

This declaration appeared to assuage Alfred's worries. 'So he's not guilty of . . . He didn't kill anyone? For a minute I thought that's what you meant, Daphne! Crikey, you know how to put the wind up someone.'

'Of course Chester's not guilty of murder – don't be absurd.' Theodora was scornful.

'No, he's not guilty of murder,' Daphne said. 'But he's not entirely innocent, either.'

'Bloody hell, Daphne –' Irene was now pacing '– can you please stop this dilly-dallying? What the bloody hell is going on?'

'It's all because of me.' When he spoke, Chester's voice was feeble and tentative. 'They . . . they were killed because of me. Because of . . . something I did. They were punished for my actions.'

Daphne exhaled with relief. Her instinct had been

correct all along. 'It's true. And after all, "Where guilt has been proven, let punishment fall." Isn't that correct, Lilian?'

It was a risk, but one that Daphne had to take. Lilian stopped picking at her gloves and looked up at Daphne. The rest of the company seemed to be holding their breath.

'I beg your pardon, Miss King?' Lilian said, no trace of wavering in her voice.

'That's what you told us just a few hours ago, Lilian. After Donald's arrest,' Daphne explained. 'It was also written on one of the postcards you sent to Chester. And of course it's a line from *A Woman of Grace and Fury*. The play that your brother wrote.'

At this, Chester crumbled entirely, involuntarily letting out a moan. He swayed, seemed about to collapse. Theodora and Cecil gripped his arms, steadying him. Alfred protested. Veronica told her brother to hush and let Daphne explain.

Theodora turned to Lilian. 'What is she talking about? What is this rubbish? *Your brother?*' Theodora's voice possessed none of the steel it had displayed just moments ago.

Lilian smirked. She sighed, strolled to the front of the stage, her back to the rest. A moment passed, during which Daphne's stomach flipped several times.

'Oh Theodora, you always did enjoy turning a blind eye to your husband's faults,' Lilian said as she turned to face the group again. 'A rather peculiar martyrdom but one you relished. Protecting him from his own weaknesses, his own failings, all these years. What exactly did you *think* all those *gifts* were about?'

Theodora stammered, 'I-I knew they were from someone from Chester's past. A woman, I thought. A woman he'd . . . wronged in some way. S-someone who wanted to make him remember, rattle him.'

'Well, in that deduction you were correct,' Lilian replied, a sudden vehemence in her voice as she looked at Chester. 'I *did* want to make you remember. I *did* want to make you scared. And Robert. And Tyrone. You'd all enjoyed your gilded existences for far too long. No consequences to your actions, no *punishment*. Meanwhile, my Russell's talent – his future – has been dead and buried for twenty years.'

In Chester's watery eyes there was a flicker of recognition, a flinch of remembrance. 'Is it true? What Daphne said? He . . . he was your *brother*?'

Alfred had been silent for quite some time and could contain himself no longer. 'I'm terribly sorry to interject, really I am, but if we've all been summoned here, we should be told the rudiments of what the blazes is going on.'

This rare demonstration of boldness from her brother made Veronica smile momentarily. She rearranged her face into a suitably sombre expression before explaining briefly, 'Chester didn't write *A Woman of Grace and Fury*: Lilian's brother did. Chester took the credit, Robert and Tyrone went along with it. Daphne worked it all out – she's been awfully clever.'

Daphne rummaged in her satchel and pulled out the photograph. She gave it to Chester.

'There. You, Tyrone, Robert. Cecil's mother had me barking up the wrong tree for a while—' Daphne was interrupted by Cecil.

'My *mother*? My mother? What on earth does my mother have to do with all of this?' he blurted out.

'Well, Cecil, that's just the thing: she has absolutely nothing to do with all of this. But for a time – well, for a time I rather thought she did. And that . . . well, that *you* did. I'll get to all that, I promise. But before I do, allow me to lay out the narrative in the plainest terms possible. I paid a visit to the Phoenix, showed this photograph to the landlord. He's been there for decades, knew who you all were – the rabble-rousers, he called you. At first he wasn't all that helpful, seemed more intent on persuading us to book a table there for New Year's Eve. It was when he looked properly at the picture that the trip became worth our while.'

Daphne pointed not to the figures in the foreground, but to the bar. There, pouring a pint, his face turned half to the side, was the barman. A man twenty or so years younger than the middle-aged Chester in the photograph. 'The landlord, Gary, is very proud of his memory for names and faces – especially those of his employees. The name tripped off his tongue immediately: Russell Rogers.'

Chester winced at the mention, while Lilian grew more righteous in her rage. 'Yes, Russell Rogers. The *true* author of the play that turned *you* into a star. That made you. The play that you *stole* from him.'

'Chester, is this . . . is this true?' Theodora's hand dropped from her husband's arm as she plaintively asked the question.

'Aha. So he hid the truth from you as well, Theodora? My, my, Chester. What a deceiver you are,' Lilian said, clearly relishing that Theodora had been unaware of the foundation of her husband's career.

Cecil, still supporting Chester, frowned. 'Chester stole your brother's play? But that was, what, twenty years ago. Why not do something before now? And why *murder*, Lilian? Surely—'

'Surely what, Cecil? Surely I should have informed the authorities back in 1912? A seventeen-year-old girl going to the police to tell them that a wealthy middle-aged man has stolen a play from her brother? I would have been laughed at. But I didn't forget. The years went by, Chester's reputation grew, and one day the penny dropped. I knew what I had to do. In this world, Cecil, one has to take control; relying on others, relying on powerful men, will only lead to disappointment at the very best.'

Alfred was still baffled. 'Why didn't your brother do something?'

'He did,' Lilian stated plainly. 'But he was a boy from Brixton, a barman with no connections, no family name, no rich friends. Nobody listened. He and I, we had only each other – and the theatre. After he clocked off at the pub, he would spend hours and hours writing. He had so many wonderful ideas, so many things to say. But he had no idea how to get his plays to anyone who mattered. Then Chester and his ... *gang* started hanging around at the pub.'

At this, Lilian's glare intensified. Chester was wringing his hands, eyes fixed on an indeterminate point on the floor. Then he spoke. 'He told us he'd written something. He was so trusting, so frank. I'd been stuck directing lacklustre productions of stultifying plays for years. I was a safe pair of hands, yes, but nobody thought I could do anything ... new or modern. I was so bored. I read the play – *A Woman of Grace and Fury* – and I knew. I knew it would be a success. It would cut through the dross and show people that I could do something worthwhile.'

'So you *took* it. He trusted you and you *stole* it.' Lilian could not allow Chester to wrest control of her brother's story from her. 'And while your star rose, he sank. He saw how successful the play was, but knew he couldn't make anyone believe it was his. The sadness, the anger, the *shame* at having trusted you . . . I watched all of it. I tried to help him. But he turned to the booze. The same old hackneyed story. And one night, too drunk to look where he was going, he was hit by a taxi on Lambeth Bridge.'

Theodora and Chester looked at Lilian. 'I'm . . . I'm s-so s-sorry, Lilian,' Chester stammered. 'If I had known it would lead to Russell's death—'

Lilian spat the words: 'Death? Oh no, Chester, Russell's not *dead*. The accident – it caused lasting damage, but it didn't kill him. No, Russell is alive, it's just that his . . . faculties aren't entirely intact. He's living in a residential home in Little Grinton. And don't even *attempt* to tell me that you didn't do it, that you would never have betrayed my brother's trust. You've had years to come clean. For a while I was stupid enough to think that you would – that you'd be honest, own up, tell everyone that it had all been a terrible misunderstanding. After a while it wouldn't have mattered, but the great Chester Harrison needed all the adulation and praise he could get from a career built on a lie. Well, now you have it. The consequences of your actions. Your friends are dead, your wife knows you're a liar ... Damned shame I didn't quite get to you, but perhaps this outcome has a touch more poetic justice.'

For a full minute nobody spoke, everyone speechless with disbelief. That Chester had committed so callous a deception. That Lilian Rogers – *Lilian Rogers* – was a double murderer.

'I suppose we should thank you, Daphne, for uncovering all of this. It seems that you prevented my husband from being murdered,' Theodora said, her voice strangely devoid of emotion. 'How on *earth* did you work it out?'

Daphne had been in something of a daze as she listened to Lilian's narrative. The anger and the malice were so raw, even after twenty years. It then occurred to her that a person so mired in anger might be entirely unpredictable and volatile. Lilian had proven herself to be vengeful, violent; what if she turned her ire now upon Daphne or any of the others? Or, on the other hand, what was there to stop the woman from attempting to flee? But then Daphne reflected that Lilian's was not an erratic anger; it was targeted, focused. And to flee now would be futile.

'Yes, do tell us, dear little Miss King. I've been wondering how you found me out – guileless luck or unearthly skill, which was it?' Lilian asked.

'Nothing unearthly about my skills, Lilian,' Daphne retorted immediately. 'In fact, I've been accused of being rather too prosaic and mundane in my methods; not enough tea-leaf-reading or Tarot cards, apparently.' She glanced at Veronica. 'For a while I was convinced that it was *you*, Cecil.'

Cecil blanched. 'Me? Why ever did you think that? What possible reason could I have had to hurt Robert – to *kill* him? He'd been so good to me; it was on his account that Chester cast me.'

Daphne wavered. She had not thought that Cecil would be entirely ignorant of his parentage. Informing the poor devil simultaneously of the existence and death of his father was not something that Daphne had bargained on including in her revelations. Daphne glanced at Veronica for reassurance. A nod was enough to tell her that she had no choice: the boy must know, one way or another.

'Cecil, I . . . Well, I must be blunt. Robert Stirling was your father,' Daphne said, her measured delivery at odds with the trepidation she felt in her chest.

His features widening, Cecil took a step backwards. 'He . . . Are you sure?'

'I believe very strongly so, yes,' Daphne said. 'Here she is in this photograph – your mother – with Robert. Along with Chester and Tyrone. I thought . . . well, I thought that you knew. That you were here to seek revenge on the man who had had an affair with your mother and then abandoned her.'

Cecil's eyes were glistening as he looked at the photograph. 'I had no idea. None at all. Is it true, Chester?'

The old man nodded, moistening his dry lips before saying, 'He regretted it – using your mother so. That's why he tracked you down, persuaded me to cast you. Which I did, willingly, gladly. We hoped that it would . . . atone for past wrongs.'

'Pah!' spat Lilian. 'A lifetime in purgatory couldn't atone for all of your past wrongs, Chester Harrison. I've no time for your sentimental prattling. Miss King, please continue.'

Striding into the centre of the stage, Daphne wanted to ensure that everyone was fully up to speed on how she had apprehended Lilian. No cloak-and-dagger smoke-and-mirrors nonsense. Good, solid, detective work.

'I knew something was amiss from the off. The mushrooms that killed Robert – *Amanita virosa* – destroying angel. It was the name, Lilian. You could have used any poisonous mushroom you liked but you chose that one. A killer who selects such a deliciously poetic name, well, that's a killer who's sending a message,' Daphne began. 'We'll return to the mushrooms later.'

Lilian smiled the smile of one whose work is finally being appreciated.

'Next, those gifts. Chester was so eager to discount them, to avoid discussing them, there had to be something in them. You'd made a mistake with one of the postcards, you see. For the most part, they'd been hand-delivered to the theatres. One, however, had been posted – from Little Grinton. Of course I had to go there.'

Lilian chuckled.

'There had to be a reason you'd posted it from there.' Lilian's chuckling subsided. She nodded silently. 'The vandal – or thief – in me stole a page from the visitors' book. But this, this it took some time to make use of – I'll come back to it later.'

'Crikey, Daphne, have you plotted this all out into a three-act structure?' Alfred asked, as bemused as he was impressed.

'Little Grinton did give me the connection I needed to the poisonous mushrooms. That helpfully loquacious chap on the desk, Francis, told us all about the infestation in the wood, and I knew I was on the right track. I also knew that your father had been a gardener, thanks to Veronica's thorough account of your early life when I first met you. Young mother and father meeting in service at a stately home. Of course people can learn about poisonous mushrooms in any manner of ways, but still. The connection was made in my mind.'

'I can't keep up with this,' Cecil murmured.

'Back to the gifts – the postcards and the pen. That pen. There was something so ornate, so deliberate about it. Cigars and wine are throwaway items. Not the pen, though. And Chester's face when he saw it, well, that confirmed that it had significance. And you choosing to murder Tyrone Bridge with it certainly added weight to my theory of its importance. Why did you steal it back from the safe?'

Daphne hadn't been able to pin down why Lilian had done this, so wanted to hear her answer.

'Yes, Tyrone threw a spanner in the works. He wasn't supposed to meet his maker quite yet, not yesterday, but needs must. Someone – Alfred, I think – mentioned the pen when we were in the bar the night before last. I knew that once the old windbag clapped eyes on it he'd start filling your ear with all sorts – you see, he knew as well as Chester did that the pen belonged to Russell. Hadn't the faintest that I was his sister, but never mind.

I needed to slow you down, Miss King. I was always going to steal the pen back; if nothing else, then just to scare Chester a little more.'

'I see,' Daphne said, glancing over to see Alfred wincing at the mention of his name in the course of a murder confession.

'Onwards though, Miss King, don't let me stop you.' Lilian gestured for her to continue.

'Tyrone's dying word, "Grace." That took me a little longer. In fact, it was Veronica who helped me with that. And the scribblings on the back of the postcards. I thought they were gnomic platitudes, no idea they were from the play. And that's it: the play's the thing, isn't it, Lilian? A little reading time at Foyles gave me everything else I needed. Firstly, you had used one of the phrases in conversation last night – quite the slip-up. Secondly, the protagonist, Isobel. I had seen the name before – in the visitors' book. An *Isobel* visiting a *Russell R.* A sentimental pseudonym for you to have used, Lilian – another slip-up. Thirdly, well, the entire French scene confirmed my suspicion that you hadn't written it, Chester.'

He looked puzzled. How had she seen through the veil kept so carefully in place for twenty years?

'Come now, an entire scene in French? And not just *any* scene; a scene drenched in nuance, empathy, not to mention the motif of sibling love. You can't speak a word of French – you and Robert made that plain when I first met you – so an entire scene in the language seemed unlikely.' Daphne suppressed a rather smug smile with difficulty. The pleasure she derived from fitting this particular piece of the puzzle was quite disproportionate to its importance in the unravelling of the crimes.

'So you see, Alfred,' Veronica chimed in, to ensure that her brother was up to speed, 'Lilian had this all plotted out from the word go. Persuaded Donald and Irene to go for the roles so that she'd have an excuse to visit the play at every stop on the tour. She needed a reason to be close to the production, close to Chester and Robert.'

'Sorry, I'm still slightly fogged,' Alfred admitted. 'I thought someone mentioned that Robert had been arguing with George – Mr Salter. Has he some part in all this?'

Aha. Daphne had been hoping that someone would pose this question. 'May I, Lilian?' She wanted to savour this revelation. 'You make an astute point, Alfred. And one which I myself was a little stumped by. But then I remembered a stain I had seen on Robert's jacket – a particularly vibrant orange stain. One which, I realised afterwards, is rather similar – if not identical – to the stain left by lily pollen. Which must be a devil to clean off if it gets on your clothes, Mr Salter?'

George Salter had been slowly and surreptitiously backing away from the group, Lilian Rogers' revelatory monologue indicating that now was the time to make an exit. Before he could, however, all attention was on him.

'Mr Salter always wears a lily in his buttonhole, an unusual choice and one which stuck in my mind. The lily pollen was transferred to Robert during the scuffle in his dressing room – the disagreement you overheard, Irene – when Mr Salter was demanding money.'

'George, you were still trying to squeeze money out of him? I *told* you not to get greedy.' Despite the preceding shocks, the voice that spoke these words prompted an audible gasp from certain members of the group. For it was the voice of Lilian Rogers.

'And I told *you*, I needed more goddamn cash.'

The gasps redoubled. Theodora appeared more shocked to hear George replying to Lilian this way than she had been to hear about her husband's decades of dishonesty.

'George? What . . . what is this? What do you mean?'

'Dora, honey, I'm sorry. It's been a ride, but it's over now,' George said gruffly. 'Rogers here's been bankrolling me the whole time. Paid me to nix your meetings in Hollywood, badmouth you around town. Persuade you to throw the towel in and come back here.'

'I needed you back in England, you see,' Lilian said. 'Couldn't have you getting too comfortable over in the good old US of A. The thought of Chester basking in the Californian sun for too long made my decision for me. It had to be done, and it had to be done soon. With my sincerest apologies, Theodora. Your career was a necessary casualty.'

'So who the bloody hell *are* you then, George?' Theodora could not quite digest the fact that she'd been quite so dramatically hoodwinked.

'A convincing actor, is what he is,' Lilian offered, 'who just happens to also be something of a hoodlum with mercifully little in the way of conscience and a penchant for dirty tricks. A colleague in New York put us in touch.'

'Lilian's been generous, and what else I got to be doin'? New York's a busted flush. I'm a resourceful fella, but LA and London weren't exactly beggin' for me to pay a visit. Who's gonna say no to an offer from a lady like Miss Rogers? Just needed a little extra cash, courtesy of Mr Stirling. You'd be surprised how easy it is to blackmail these guys. So many skeletons in their closets they barely got space for their fancy suits.' George was enjoying his new role, out of the shadows. He had ambled towards a gravestone, upon which he now rested his hands.

'One more thing I couldn't quite work out, if you'd be so kind?' Daphne was looking at Lilian. 'How did you get the mushrooms to Robert? Did you disguise yourself and join the staff at the sandwich shop at Piccadilly Circus tube, the one that Robert went to every morning?'

Lilian laughed mirthlessly. 'Heavens no, Miss King. Nothing so elaborate as that. I simply offered him the sandwiches – and he simply accepted them. Robert Stirling was a man who took unquestioningly from life – took whatever he could, whenever he could.'

Daphne surveyed the scene. Theodora, her features contorted in dismay. Chester, leaning heavily on Cecil. Irene had folded her arms, as though bored by proceedings. Alfred was ruffling his hair, his face even paler than it had been earlier. Lilian, in contrast with the others, appeared disquietingly serene. Content, even. The retribution she had sought was complete.

Veronica touched Daphne's arm. 'When did Marklow say he'd be here?'

During her telephone call with Marklow, Daphne had suggested that he and some colleagues from the station might want to revisit the theatre that evening. She had disclosed her suspicion that the perpetrator would be there. The perpetrator and her accomplice, poised to commit the final murder. Marklow had sighed wearily before reluctantly agreeing to one final trip to 'that bloody theatre'.

A smile had crept across Lilian's face. She was looking at Chester. 'I don't care that they'll send me to prison, Chester. My brother has had justice. Finally. What is it that you've accomplished?'

34

The next day, Christmas Eve, Daphne sat at the desk in her bedroom. She had slept deeply and dreamlessly but not for long. The events of the past few days had weighed heavily on her mind, and, as the clock downstairs on Mrs Booth's mantelpiece struck seven, Daphne had already been writing for three hours. She had wired Martin Halliday a brief precis of the previous night's events so as to make it into the morning paper, and now her more detailed account was ready for the evening edition.

She put the cap back on her pen and rested it on her notebook. The elation that she'd felt yesterday was ebbing away. She had unmasked a murderer, revealed long-hidden secrets, but the fruits of her investigation gave her little joy. For lives had been ruined, some lost. Lilian would be sentenced. Theodora's world had been turned upside down. Even Cecil had been forced to confront the true nature of the man who was his father.

She glanced at her watch. A few hours until she would have to board the train to Slough. Her nieces and nephew would demand entertaining, her mother would pester her about her marriage prospects. Daphne closed her eyes. Sherlock Holmes hadn't had to contend with this sort of thing.

There was a tentative knock at the door. Mrs Booth really ought to confine herself to more sensible hours. What the devil could she want now?

'Visitor for you, Miss King! I'll thank you to tell your acquaintances that we run a house where seven o'clock callers are *not* appreciated,' Mrs Booth said, her tone sharp.

'Yes, Mrs Booth, I'm coming,' Daphne grumbled, heaving herself from her chair.

Downstairs, Veronica stood on the doorstep in an oversized deep-green overcoat. 'King, I haven't been able to sleep. No amount of gin has helped. What say you get dressed and we go for a walk?'

In the frosty December air, the sun barely crawling out from behind heavy clouds, with Veronica Burford marching along by her side, Daphne's mind felt clear again. She would think of that walk when, four days later, Martin Halliday called her into his office and gracefully agreed to her request that she retire Dear Susan and join the crime desk. The walk would be on her mind the following year when she and Veronica sat in the stalls to watch a revival of *A Woman of Grace and Fury*. The furore around the murders had sparked renewed interest in the play and its true author; the name Russell Rogers featured prominently on the posters outside the theatre on Shaftesbury Avenue. She would also think of the walk when she visited Lilian Rogers in prison to give her a copy of the play's programme.

Right now, however, Veronica Burford was suggesting that they make their way to Soho. After all, it was five o'clock somewhere in the world. And it was Christmas Eve.

Acknowledgements

Huge thanks to all at Vintage for their care and expertise: Alex Russell, Polly Dorner, Mia Quibell-Smith, Kate Neilan and all who have worked behind the scenes on bringing *Murder at the Theatre Royale* to bookshelves. Thank you to my friends and family for all their support. And thank you to Rachel, of course, for all things.

ADA MONCRIEFF

Murder Most Festive

Christmas Eve, 1938. The Westbury family and assorted
friends have gathered for another legendary celebration
at their beautiful country house. The champagne flows,
the silverware sparkles and upstairs the rooms
are ready for their occupants.

But one bed will lie empty that night. On Christmas
morning, David Campbell-Scott is found dead
in the snow. There's a pistol beside him
and only one set of footprints.

Yet something doesn't seem right to amateur sleuth
Hugh Gaveston. Campbell-Scott had just returned
from overseas with untold wealth – why would he
kill himself? Hugh sets out to investigate . . .